A Carpet of

Violets & Clover

Short Stories, Personal Essays &

Poems

Jenny Zimmer

Our Magical Summer

We played on the bluff where thick moss grew on tree trunks

And violets carpeted the ground.

We twisted white clover blossoms into necklaces and bracelets

And wore them proudly.

We swung on the wooden gate that opened into the barnyard

*And we chewed on the mint leaves that grew wild along the
fence row.*

We dipped our toes into the cool brown water of the pond

*And we watched the horses swish away the flies with their long
tails.*

Sometimes we sat on the trunk of a tree

That grew perpendicularly out over the creek bed,

And our bare feet danced in the air over the bubbling water.

That summer was truly magical for us.

Every day was an adventure that we thought would never end

Yet they always ended when we heard Aunt May calling

To come in and wash up for supper.

To Al, who was my champion and the love of my life.

Contents

Short Stories

A Tall Tale

He wore a red golf shirt, drinking a beer, and smoking a cigarette as he held court at the table next to us.

Enjoying our margaritas in the balmy late afternoon on the patio of a neighborhood restaurant, we paid only scant attention to the conversation at the other table.

But my interest in their conversation perked up when I heard, "I was at Jerry Lee's house a lot. He had a big assed house with a huge swimming pool. In the middle of the pool was an island that rose up out of the water and there was a big white piano sitting on that island!"

The guy in the gray tee shirt set his beer on the table and looked intently at red shirt. "Whoa… you mean he actually had a real piano in the pool? Now that's hard to believe."

"Yeah, he sure as hell does!"

"Well, what does he do with it… just swim around the island and enjoy looking at the piano?"

The guy in the red shirt took a long swig of his beer and lit another cigarette before he answered.

"Nah, one time he came home while we were sitting around the pool and, in typical Jerry Lee style, he swaggered over to a wall switch which, when he flipped it up, raised a bridge up and out of the water, leading to the piano. It was the damnedest thing I'd ever seen."

Gray shirt just shook his head and motioned to the bartender that he needed a fresh beer.

Red shirt sat back, crossing one foot over his other knee and silently studied his black and white, soft spiked golf shoe while gray shirt and the other man, who was wearing a button-down collar white dress shirt, looked on and waited for the story to continue.

Raising his beer in a mock toast, red shirt said, "Jerry Lee trotted across the bridge and stood at the piano grinning at us as he yelled over asking what we'd like to hear him play."

"Of course I said I'd like to hear 'Great Balls of Fire' and Jerry Lee whooped as his hands crashed down on the keys."

The beer flowed and smoke drifted up from our cigarettes as we sat, drinking and smoking as he gave us a full concert from the middle of his pool."

Now white shirt spoke, "You're full of bull – why would we think you've ever been to Jerry Lee's house?"

Gray shirt shifted around in his chair and nodded, "Yeah, you're full of it all right!"

Red shirt adjusted the ball cap he was wearing and replied, "Hell man, I was part of the family cause I was married to Jerry Lee's cousin, a sister to the cousin he married."

Shaking his head, gray shirt motioned to the cute blond bartender for another Bud Light and muttered, "Well, I'll be damned!"

Neighbors

Our new neighbors are a lot noisier than I like. They play their music quite loud and sometimes they sing; even their dog joins in, wailing and howling even louder and more annoyingly than the neighbors themselves.

So, what can I do?

Well, I decided that a taste of their own medicine might work, so I cranked up my Sirius XM radio, tuned to Channel 59, Willie's Road House, and sang along with Hank Williams as he decried his lonesome life. Sad songs – one after another. I sang them all and quite loudly too.

I was sounding pretty good, or so I thought, till a loud knock sounded at my front door and pulled me out of my moment. The policeman who stood there announced that he had come because of a complaint from the neighbors about the noise.

Hapless

Dick was surprised to find, quite by accident, that he was often considered to be "hapless" by his friends. Not knowing what the word hapless meant, he looked it up in the dictionary to find that it essentially meant 'unlucky or unhappy'. He couldn't really understand how they could see him in that way… he was neither unhappy nor unlucky.

In fact, he often sat in his recliner at night thinking of his life and about how lucky he was. He was lucky that his wife had decided to run away with the mailman and was no longer around to criticize and admonish him all day long.

He also felt lucky that his company had decided, after a lot of years, to eliminate his job and let him go.

Now he was free to sit on the porch with his morning coffee, brewed just the way he liked it and with sugar and cream. He listened to the birds chirping merrily while he watched the traffic go by. Yes, it was noisy on the porch in the morning, but he found it soothing and always thought how lucky he was to be able to sit here day after day and enjoy it.

So now he wondered… why would his friends think of him as hapless or unlucky/unhappy when he was probably luckier and happier than any of them? His life was perfect!

Happy Birthday to Me!

Gina woke to sunlight streaming through the dingy window. She realized that today was her birthday; she was 20 years old. But there would be no birthday celebration today; things were so tight for her family and everyone else and food was not easily obtained, especially something as special as a birthday cake or ice cream.

She laid there for a while, watching the sunlight play on the wall and the shapes of leaves that shifted and danced across it, moving smoothly to some silent melody. Glancing at the clock, she realized that it was only 6:30 AM and her normal time to get up was 7:00 AM, so she had a half-hour to just lie there and think.

Stretching slowly, she let her mind wander. She thought about how different things were now from just a few years ago. She thought about when she was a teenager and how things had been so good; her life had been so carefree then. Food had been plentiful and special things such as birthday cakes were always available. She wondered, not for the first time, how things could have changed so much in those few years?

She hadn't paid much attention to politics or any of the things her parents had worried about when she was fifteen. Now she wished that she had because maybe, just maybe, she could better understand how such dramatic change could occur in such a short time. Now, just thinking about all the changes made her feel sad. She also felt scared just thinking about what the future might bring.

There had been a presidential election 5 years ago and voters had elected a liberal candidate who favored growing the government so that it would take control of more and more areas of the lives of citizens. At that time, there were also several indications that many people age 30 and under favored a socialistic form of government, and therefore they favored big government. Since she hadn't been old enough to vote in that election, she hadn't thought too much about what the election might mean to people like her family. Now, just 5 years later, everyone was feeling the sting of changes that were bringing hard times to most families.

Crime was out of control; police were under siege in many big cities; government spending was increasing and beginning to affect and monitor the everyday life of everyone; and people no longer wanted to work, they sat on their porches every day, drinking coffee or beer and smoking cigarettes. They had no ambition, no drive, and no expectations.

Birth rates were increasing and the government was now contemplating ways to harness/control this population explosion, even to the extent of sterilization for females who were impaired in some way and females over 14 years of age after two pregnancies. And of course, getting a free abortion at any age was a common form of birth control. This was scary, and for people like Gina and her younger siblings, threatening to their futures.

But there had recently been another election and voters, scared of what was happening to this country, had voted for a more conservative and forward-thinking president. But... was it too late to turn things around and bring the country and its citizens back to prosperity? Could people be inspired to seek jobs, to work in factories, to return the schools and churches to their former position of teaching, encouraging and motivating? It would take some time, but with everyone working together, it could be accomplished. So... there was hope for the future after all!

Now, hearing a slight noise, Gina turned her head toward the bed that stood against the far wall. She saw that her six-year-old sister Rey had climbed out of the bed and was now helping her little brother Xander climb down to the floor beside her. The two of them padded quietly over to Gina.

"Hi Gee," whispered Rey as she smiled shyly. Xander reached up and patted Gina's arm as he smiled up at her.

"Gee, will you tell us one of those lies like you told us before?"

Gina was puzzled, "Lies? I've never told you lies. I just told you stories of how things used to be."

Rey said, "But our teacher told us that some grown-ups would tell us lies about how things used to be, but it was all just lies. We're not supposed to listen to these lies."

Gina's heart ached for these little ones.

Then, brightening, Rey added, "Yes, tell us a story. We won't tell anybody that you told us."

Tearfully Gina pulled them up beside her, looked at the clock, and began to tell them about how she had gone to school, had been able to be outside, playing with other kids, and making up games. She told them how the teachers had taught them how to do math in their heads and to write in cursive. She told them about the thrill of accomplishment.

She told them about the food that her mother prepared for them and about how the family all sat together in their home, eating meals, talking, laughing, and making plans for vacations or trips to visit Grandma in Florida. She told them about the things she learned in school, how the country was founded, the constitution, the Civil War, World Wars I and II, and the significance of each of these occurrences.

Rey and Xander were spellbound and soaked it all in. Then the morning bell that signaled time to get up and dressed for the day sounded and startled them from the lovely world that Gina described back to the dull, regimented routine that awaited them each day.

Silently Gina prayed that these young children and others would soon see that these stories were true and not lies as some today would have them believe.

And a Pleasant Good Morning to You Too!

When Tom arrived at his mom's house yesterday morning for their daily visit and coffee, he found her in a very unusual state. Instead of the neatly dressed, sweet-smelling woman he was used to seeing at the door, he stopped short when he saw the woman who met him when he walked into the house.

This stranger was still in her nightgown and slippers. She had a ratty-looking old sweater thrown over her shoulders and her hair was sticking up on one side and laying completely flat on the other, giving her a strange lop-sided look. He stared at the woman before him. She was a complete wreck and frankly, she looked a little wild.

"Mom, what's going on? Why aren't you dressed? Are you O.K?"

"Oh Tom, something terrible has happened! I don't know what to do... I've lost my 45!"

"What do you mean 'you've lost your 45'? I didn't even know you had one."

"Don't be silly, of course you did. I've had for a long time, ever since you were a little boy. I didn't get it out very often, but I've always had it near me. Now I don't know where it is."

She had tears in her eyes as she looked up at him and silently pleaded for his help. Tom knew he needed to help her, but first he needed to calm her down. With his arms around her, he assured her that they would find it. He would help her look. After all, it had to be somewhere in the house, didn't it?

Wiping her eyes with the corner of her sweater and, with a pitiful little smile, she squeezed his hand and nodded.

"Now mom, where was it the last time you saw it?"

"It was right where I always kept it, in the bottom of my underwear drawer."

"Well, since it's not there now, did you maybe put it somewhere else?"

"Why would I ever do that?"

This conversation was going nowhere, and Tom felt himself beginning to lose patience. He asked when she had last had it out and when she had last used it. She looked up at him as if he were such a slow thinker and she said, "You know I only played it on special occasions… so the last time I had it out would have been at Christmas. Don't you remember? I played it then."

Slowly the light bulb came on in Tom's head – played it? She *played* it?

Then he began laughing and grabbed his mom in a big bear hug. "Your 45! You're talking about your Elvis record, aren't you?"

She nodded yes and pulled back to look up at him, puzzled at his words. What on earth had he thought she was talking about?

Tom walked over to the big old stereo and pulled open the drawer where the record player sat. There, on the turntable, sat the small 45 RPM record of Elvis singing 'Love Me Tender'.

Holding it up for his mom to see, he said, "Here it is!"

A huge smile blossomed across her face as she clapped her hands together and stared at the lost 45. "Oh, my! You've found my lost 45. I never thought to look there. I'm so relieved and happy!" she said.

Just Buying a Big Bud

I was really just standing there, looking around, killing time as I waited for the young woman at the self-check register to finish so I could check out and head home when I noticed the lady behind me seemed to be very interested in me. She was looking at me and I had a distinct feeling that she was sizing me up. Feeling a little embarrassed because I had just stopped at Meijer's on my way home from work and was in my dirty work clothes, I quickly turned around and tried to look like I was interested in my shopping basket.

God, that young woman in front of me was slow! It seemed to take her forever before she finally picked up her two bags and moved away from the register. I touched the screen to begin the checkout process then picked up my one item, a quart size of Bud Light, and ran it across the screen. Nothing happened. I ran it across the screen again, more slowly this time. Still, nothing happened. Not wanting to look around to see what kind of line was behind me, I searched for an attendant.

I motioned to the young lady wearing the Meijer's vest that I needed her assistance and she, with a smile, walked over to me. She had to punch in some kind of code and reset the machine. While she was punching in numbers and sliding her card over the screen, I turned, without thinking and there she was, the same lady that had been eyeing me earlier. This time she gave me a bright smile and kind of nodded her head. I just looked at her, not knowing how to respond.

Holy cow… was she flirting with me? I don't think so. Maybe she was smiling because I was standing there holding my big quart-sized can of Bud Light and was probably looking a little anxious to boot. So, not knowing what to do, I didn't do anything other than turn back toward the attendant. Thankfully, she had finished her number punching and card swiping ministrations and she indicated that I could now scan my item. I quickly scanned the Bud Light, put my money in the slot, grabbed my change and hot-footed it out of the store without looking around.

As I walked to the far end of the parking lot where my new Jeep Cherokee sat, I thought about that lady who had been looking me over and now I smiled. I wondered if she thought because I was in dirty clothes and had nothing but a big can of beer in my cart that I was someone who was down-on-my-luck and had just managed to gather enough coins to buy a big beer. As I got in my new Jeep and revved up the engine, I wondered, what kind of world is it that a guy can't even buy a big Bud Light to marinate his mets and brats before grilling them for his tennis buddies after our game tonight?

Just Like She Said

The scenery certainly was beautiful – just like she said it was.

The air was fresh even if at this elevation it took a little more effort to breathe; she had also warned me about that on the drive up here.

I hadn't really wanted to see this kind of scenery – to look at areas where trees were not to be seen and the air, although fresh, was dry and made my nose feel funny. There was also no water to be seen, no hint of an ocean breeze, or the coconut scent of suntan lotion. There was no laughter or excited cries coming from a beach volleyball game, and certainly there were no bikini-clad women parading down the beach, kicking up the cooling spray with their long legs and bare feet.

This vacation was not exactly what I had hoped for when we began planning a trip, but she had told me how much I'd enjoy it and how glad I'd be to experience a different kind of trip. Oh yeah, It was different, all right.

So here I am in Utah, smiling for the camera and looking relaxed and happy. But as I stand here, exactly where I was told to stand, I can't help but wonder...

Why did she have to literally twist my arm to get me here? I would have come anyway, just to make her happy and maybe, just maybe, to satisfy my curiosity to see if it really was as beautiful as she said it would be.

My Quiet Neighbor

She was quiet and we seldom saw her going out or coming in. We thought of her as 'an old maid', but she probably wasn't even forty.

We would often hear music coming from her apartment and, although we never saw anyone, sometimes we heard a soft knocking on her door late in the evening and suspected that she had a gentleman visiting her.

Imagine our surprise when one day we found three used condoms lying on the hall runner where they had obviously fallen from her trash can as she carried it out to empty it into the dumpster.

But... three condoms? We'd only heard one knock on her door in the past week... hmmmm. That makes me wonder just how often she empties that trash can anyway.

Oliver's Car

We squeezed into Oliver's car and set off for the funeral. The car was small and we were really jammed into the back seat.

First of all, I'm not a good back seat rider so I was uncomfortable from the start – expecting my stomach to start rolling at any second.

"Give me some air," I said as I tried to reach across three people to find and turn the window crank. They were all talking and no one paid any attention to me.

I was beginning to feel hot and sweaty so this time, I raised my voice and cried out, "AIR – AIR – I need air! I'm going to be sick." And with that, the girl next to the window rolled it halfway down so that air whooshed into the car and saved me from total disgrace.

I was relieved, color came back into my cheeks and I felt better. I looked around at my companions for the first time since getting into the car with them.

"WHAT!"

Who were these people? Whose funeral procession were we in?

Oh my God, I've followed the wrong group out of the church and am going to the funeral of someone I don't even know.

Oh well, I wasn't planning anything for the rest of the afternoon anyway, and what the heck, they may just have a wonderful life celebration party and who knows, maybe some cute guys will be there. Now I can handle that!

But I do wonder… WHO IS OLIVER?

Mystery in the Hen House

The only grandpa I knew was actually my dad's stepfather. He was not a very nice man, and he always complained about us kids when we visited on Sunday afternoons. He was also quite stingy and would be upset when grandma told him to give us something from the garden or, heaven forbid, from the fruit trees.

Last Sunday, grandma told us that grandpa had started sleepwalking. She followed him through the house into the yard and then straight to the garden. He grabbed a bucket and began picking beans, okra and tomatoes, filling the bucket full.

Then he walked into the hen house, creating a cackling mess of chickens when he interrupted their night, and he started putting vegetables into the nests. When he finished, he wiped his hands down the side of his legs, then went back into the house, where he climbed into bed and started to snore.

The next morning, he was beside himself when he went to gather eggs and found only vegetables in the nests!

Grandma never told him how they got there!

My Surprise

The water really didn't seem that deep. When he walked in, it only came up to his hips. I was very afraid of water but, when I saw that it wasn't deep, I felt that I could also walk into it without feeling panic. So I did. The water came up to my hips, then my waist and I began feeling concerned; what had I gotten myself into? The water kept rising and soon was up to my chest, but by then I was standing in front of him. Maybe I would be ok after all.

I strangled on the water as my head went under and came up coughing and struggling. I grabbed his arm when I came up and held on for dear life, coughing and kicking my feet as I lost my balance and started to fall back into the water.

Speaking softly, he said to me, "I baptize you in the name of Jesus."

A Very Hot Wedding

"I'm sure glad I don't have a lot of clothes on," the bride whispered to her twin, who was also her maid of honor.

Sweat trickled down her neckline and into her cleavage, leaving a snail-like trail that ended somewhere below the lacy strapless top. It was a hot day to be sure; no breeze stirred the big sycamore tree that framed the area where guests were seated as they waited for wedding to begin.

The bride and maid of honor wore dresses that were identical in style, but one was white and the other one blue. A lack of jewelry made them each feel a little cooler but not by much. They turned to smile at each other, each with their own thoughts.

I'll be happy when I can get out of this dress and grab a beer, the maid of honor thought.

The bride's brow pulled into a frown as she thought... *with the sun shining through the tree leaves and directly onto the spot where she would be standing to say her vows, maybe her idea of not wearing any underwear hadn't been the great idea she's thought earlier.*

The music began, the maid of honor stood in place, the groom waited, and waited, and waited for the bride to appear, not knowing that while they were waiting, she was frantically trying to get her mother to give her the panties she wore. Her mother refused.

Yes, the weather was really hot and the guests uncomfortable, but none so much as the bride who was just anxious to get this over with and get her underwear on.

One October Night

One cool and dreary October night, I lost my glasses and found a heart-stopping adventure.

You see, I had pulled my car onto the side of the road to look at the map in the seat beside me. I reached for my reading glasses, which always hung from the rear view mirror, as I unfolded the map, then looked up from the map when my fingers grasped only air... no glasses. I checked on the floor and all around the seat but no glasses. Where were they?

Suddenly, there was the sound of something solid hitting the back fender. Looking into the side mirror, I saw a human form making its way slowly along the side of the car, heading toward where I sat in the front seat. It was just starting to be dusk and soon, I would be surrounded by total darkness.

I quickly checked to make certain all the doors were locked, but then I lowered the window one inch when the person rapped their knuckles against the glass.

"What do you want?" I asked the form which I now recognized as a small woman or large girl.

"Sir, I've been walking for a long, long time and I'm hungry. Could you possibly have any food in your car?" The face that was pressed against the glass looked to be about 14-15 years old and, despite the ragged condition of her clothes and the old blanket that she carried, she looked like a decent person. Deciding to take a chance as my fear had subsided somewhat and anxiety had filled its place, I passed a Kit-Kat bar, a bag of pretzels, and an apple out the window toward her reaching hand. She smiled, mumbled a thank you, and slowly walked away.

I sat there very still and wondered if I had imagined this encounter. I looked at the map that lay there on the seat and at my cap, which was thrown next to the map and I felt calmed by the normalcy of the scene.

But, where the hell were my glasses? Not anywhere around me for sure. Oh well, I'll get my extra ones from my suitcase in the trunk.

Looking around carefully and seeing no one or anything that was out of the ordinary, I got out of the car, opened the trunk and reached for my bag. Then I noticed it... my glasses were lying there, opened up as if someone had just taken them off. How did they get into the trunk? I'd had them in the car with me when I began the trip.

Could that strange girl have anything to do with my glasses? I guess I'll never know.

Shady Lane

Shady Lane was aptly named since the street was peppered with lovely old Tudor houses that sat on large manicured lots with trees that stretched up tall and stately, providing shade that invited lazy afternoons in a hammock.

Early that morning, around 8:00 AM, to be exact, a large boom truck pulled into the drive of the last house on the right, and crews began setting things up for the job ahead of them. The crew's supervisor walked up the steps and rang the doorbell. When no one answered, he tried calling the phone number listed on his work order. No answer there either.

Then, knowing that the customer had indicated the work was to be done whether or not they were home, he instructed the crew to begin the process of taking down the tree. The tree was large and beautiful and he privately thought it was a shame that the owners wanted to take it down but... that's what the customer had paid them to do.

That evening there were two very unhappy homeowners on Shady Lane. One was irritated that the tree he wanted removed was still standing and the other was stunned and angry when he arrived home to find that his beautiful elm tree was gone!

Shelter from the Storm

The old house was a non-descript shade of gray with windows that were dull and streaked with years of rain and grit. I wondered if I should peek through one of the windows and try to see what was inside before I opened the door. Nah, I'll just do it. Here goes...

The door wasn't locked and opened easily when I pushed on it. The smell that stung my nose and almost took my breath away as I stepped inside was awful! It smelled like dead animals, rotten wood, discarded food, dirty clothes and everything else you can imagine, all rolled into one god-awful odor. But it was a terrible night outside and I needed shelter so, pushing to open the door further and using two fingers to pinch my nose so that the smell became almost bearable, I cautiously entered the house.

I looked around quickly as the heavy door closed behind me and the floor creaked under my feet as I moved from the dim hall into the room that was visible through the opening off the hallway. It appeared to be a big room. I could tell from the little light that came through the big window that the room was filled with furniture, cobwebs and lots of dust.

I stiffened as I felt the air around me move and something brushed against my ankle. I stifled a scream, unsure if I wanted anyone to know I was there. Oh boy, what a night! First getting lost, then finding this house

25

which I thought would provide shelter from the downpour outside.

Moving cautiously across to look out the gritty window, I stopped suddenly, hearing something. I stood still and listened intently. There it was again... voices, soft and rumbling and, I thought, sounding a little frantic. But, being curious, I started walking toward the voices and then, without warning, the room I was in opened into a large dining hall where tables, chairs, and people were gathered as if for an event.

The wall sconces were glowing with a soft light which brought out the beautiful gowns worn by the ladies and emphasized the handsomeness of their partners. When I entered the room, everyone turned to look at me and the room grew very quiet. Then, as one voice, they yelled, "Happy Halloween!"

I stood there, totally surprised and I'm sure I felt something wet and warm trickle down my leg.

Was it the End or a New Beginning?

"Dammit Kelly, can't you do anything right? You must be too stupid to remember how I like my shirts folded, is that it?"

Kelly stood quietly at the foot of the bed and watched Ben refold the shirt she had just ironed and carefully folded. The large suitcase lay open on the bed and although it was already stuffed, he managed to put the shirt in before closing it.

His critical words stung like icy pellets as they hit her, and she quickly raised a hand to brush away the unbidden tears that came with his scorn. She watched Ben's actions in stunned disbelief; her marriage of six years had just ended. Ben was leaving her.

She tried to summon some regret over their failed marriage but could only feel something that felt like relief; relief that it had finally come to an end and relief that Ben would be gone from her life and with his leaving would take away the stress and hurt that he had so casually brought into their daily lives.

Standing at the window, she saw him sling his jacket over the pile of books in the passenger seat, then settle behind the steering wheel and put on the expensive sunglasses that he felt defined him.

In a motion that sealed his decision to leave, he pushed the start button and the motor on his sports car roared to life. He backed down the drive and, without a backward glance, drove away. Just like that.

A mixture of emotions coursed through Kelly as she stood looking at the empty driveway, her arms wrapped around her middle as if she were holding herself together. In a way, she was doing just that.

Was it the end or a new beginning?

Three Wishes

A hot shower and clean underwear made me feel like a new man after a speeding ticket, a lost wallet and then spending the rest of the night in a stinky, crowded, noisy holding cell at the police station while they verified my identity.

Throwing a sport coat over my shoulder, I headed out for steak, a beer and, if luck was with me, the chance to hook up with a hot-looking chick in jeans that screamed for attention. After the last 24 hours, I was tired of cops.

Opening the door of my favorite steak house, I walked into the pulsing beat of music and the soft glow of lights. I found my favorite spot, not quite at the bar and not quite away from the dance floor, and my favorite waitress immediately brought me a drink.

I saw her within seconds; she was tall, slender, and sexy. She was quite obviously eyeing me. The invitation was clear.

We danced and she hummed in my ear as her hand drew little circles on my shoulder. Suddenly she said, "I came here with friends but they left a while ago so I need a ride home. Could you give me a lift?"

When we arrived at her condo, she asked if I would like to come in and of course I said yes. As soon as we got inside, she showed me where the brandy and glasses were kept and asked if I would pour.

She removed her jacket, revealing a lot of skin and a short, lacy camisole top over low riding jeans. I saw it immediately… the large purple bruise that went from her waist down her hip and disappeared into her jeans.

"Wow that's some bruise, what happened?"

"Oh that, it's from the utility belt that I wear at work. It's kinda heavy and bangs against my hip all day."

"Really, what are you, a lineman, or electrician, or something like that?"

Smiling sweetly she said, "No, nothing like that… I'm a police officer.

Looked like my three wishes had come true tonight, but maybe I should have specified that no cops would be involved.

The Missing Dog

His name was Lanslow and that's exactly what he was called by everyone mainly because there was no plausible nickname for Lanslow, well maybe Lanny.

As he walked slowly home from work that day, old Mrs. Abbot came out to greet him and, as usual, to chat a bit. He didn't mind spending time with her, she was alone and, he suspected, pretty lonely. But today Mrs. Abbot seemed distracted and even a little sad. She just wasn't herself.

After preliminary courtesies had been exchanged, he asked her if something was wrong, if she wasn't feeling well or if something had happened to make her so unlike her generally happy self. She looked up at this handsome young man who obviously was interested in what she had to say and told this story.

"My niece came by to visit me today and she brought her dog, Reba with her. She, the dog, was such a sweetheart and, well, so is Anne my niece. Anyway, when Anne took Reba out to pee, she, the dog, not my niece, took off after a squirrel and before we knew it, she, the dog, had just disappeared. Poof! Just like that – gone! It's a mystery where she could be… we've looked everywhere. Anne had to leave and she was just heartbroken. I promised to keep looking. Maybe you can help me look?"

31

As she'd been talking, Lanslow was thinking – *now what have I gotten myself into – a missing dog, an old lady who is upset... there goes my quiet evening.*

So, instead of continuing on his way, he started looking everywhere he could think of and after an hour of searching, he saw Reba trot around the corner of Mrs. Abbot's house and, he could swear that she, not Mrs. Abbot, had a smile on her face.

Mrs. Abbot was happy, he was relieved and Reba wasn't telling anybody where she'd been or why she was smiling.

The Long Drive Home

It had been a long day... in fact, it had seemed longer than usual and she was feeling very tired.

The day hadn't started well. The car didn't want to start even though the weather didn't seem cold enough to cause that to happen. No doubt she was going to have to shell out $95 for the new battery the mechanic said she needed and that was money she'd saved for her next semester's tuition.

Getting a college degree was important to her; so important in fact that she was working two jobs so that she could pay her tuition. During the day, three days a week, from 8:30 to 4:30, she was an administrative assistant to a high-level stock broker and then, from 5:30 to 10:00 she worked at the local Texas Roadhouse where she was able to make good tips as a server. When she finished her shift at Texas Roadhouse, she still had a 35-minute drive home.

Every evening was the same... after kicking her shoes off and getting into soft sweats, she would settle down to study for one and a half hours before heading to bed, exhausted, around 1:00 AM.

When she left work that night, she noticed that it had gotten much colder. As she drove home, she thought that it would probably be even colder tomorrow morning and wondered if the car would start then and if not, what her options would be.

Suddenly the car skidded a bit and jerked her back to full consciousness. Her mind swung from thoughts of the cold weather and her car not starting to the road that had suddenly become very slippery in spots.

She slowed to a crawl and relaxed a bit as the car held to the road. She leaned over to switch her radio to a different station, one that had more lively music and would keep her fully alert as she drove.

All at once, without warning, the car lurched across the road and then seemed to float down into the shallow ravine that paralleled the road. The car gently came to rest on an incline, its headlights beaming up into the sky. And, into the quiet night, Patsy Cline belted out 'Walking After Midnight'.

A Certain Feeling

It could probably be called a dump or at least a 'last resort', but motels with a lighted Vacancy sign were few and far between on the lonely stretch of highway.

It seemed like we'd been on the road for hours instead of the two hours we'd actually been driving.

The room smelled like stale smoke and something else that wasn't quite identifiable. However, overall it looked pretty clean and the plumbing worked, so it would do.

Walt suggested I lie down and rest while he showered. I must have dozed off when suddenly the bed started moving under me and there was a strange whirring noise close to me. Then I felt a weight on me and I heard, "Can you feel it?"

My fuzzy brain wanted to shout, "Of course, I can feel it, and you're lying on top of me, for Pete's sake!"

But I didn't say anything as I woke fully and looked around to see what was going on. Then I saw it, a little box on the table next to the bed that said, "Insert a quarter (25 cents) and push the Start button for vibration."

Fortunately for me, Walt didn't have many quarters.

The Lady in Pink

He saw her walk in but hardly gave it a thought except to wonder briefly what she was doing here. She looked out of place in her soft, flowing pink outfit.

Her blonde hair touched her shoulders and swayed as she moved across the room toward him. She walked a little unsteadily in her high heels.

"Hey Jim, are you still with us or just girl watching?" His friends laughed as he, picking up his beer, turned back to the table where they sat.

But the woman in pink lace seemed to have taken up residence in Jim's mind and it took all his restraint not to turn back to see where she was sitting.

Then, unable to resist any longer, he stole a look over his shoulder and was shocked to see that she was standing only a few feet from him and looking intently at him. Caught off guard, he turned completely away from his friends to stare at the woman now standing right in front of him.

She was dressed entirely in pink and wore gold high-heeled sandals. She nervously clutched a wide-brimmed straw hat that had a pink ribbon trailing from a large pink flower perched on the crown.

He couldn't say a word, only stared. The tight shiny skin on her face, prominent cheek bones and the pouty pink lips indicated that she had made some attempt to appear younger than she was, but her sad eyes with their flirty false lashes and her hands with their long pink nails showed that she was probably several years older than he had thought when he saw her walk in. She looked like an old movie star and he was reminded of the movie, 'Sunset Boulevard'.

She walked closer and reaching out, laid her hand on his shoulder. His friends stopped talking and watched the scene playing out in front of them.

She smiled sadly down at him, squeezed his shoulder a bit and, with tears in her eyes, whispered, "Why didn't you come back? I waited and waited and I've looked everywhere. I've missed you so!"

He couldn't speak, just looked up at her and shook his head. After what seemed a long time, she turned and walked slowly away, her pink skirt swaying around her ankles as she moved.

The silence at the table was uncomfortable. Then someone spoke, "Hey guys, are we playing cards or not… Jim it's your turn to deal."

The Bracelet

Sybil Potts was somewhat of an enigma... who she was, where she came from, and how she came to live in this small town was a mystery. Oh, not that anyone cared anymore but nonetheless, the mystery remained.

Young, fortyish at most, stylish, charming, and clever, Sybil was married to Gerard Potts, who was fondly known to everyone in town as Pottsy. He was a professor, author and local historian who traveled frequently, speaking on his various interests. That he was at least twenty-five years older that Sybil was just an unimportant fact, which bothered no one, least of all themselves.

No one knew exactly where, when, or even how they had met. She just showed up as Pottsy's bride when he returned from one of his speaking tours that had kept him in Kentucky and Tennessee for several weeks.

Sybil won the hearts of everyone she met. She was, it seemed, the perfect mate for someone of Pottsy's stature and temperament. Their affection for each other was obvious and, even enviable.

It was the time of the year for the Garden Club's annual event, which featured a flower show, dinner and dance. It was the social event of the season and drew people from the surrounding towns. Tickets were sold quickly and were coveted, especially since Sybil had accepted the chairmanship of the committee planning the event.

Not only was she a master at planning and executing a big event like this, but she was also somewhat of a style-setter, even without realizing it. Her innate sense of style made others seek to find a similar look for themselves.

Hers was a simple, elegant look with a minimum of jewelry. Her hair was short and cut in a style that flattered her somewhat round face. Her makeup was flawless, giving her almost too large nose a slimmer look and enhancing her unusual almost almond-shaped gray eyes. While not striking, she would definitely be considered a 'looker'. Pottsy took great pride in showing off his wife and people were instantly charmed.

There was one thing about her that stirred curiosity though. She wore, on her left wrist, a wide cuff bracelet. She was never seen without it, in fact.

The bracelet, fashioned with a combination of a polished and hammered metal of some sort, was eye-catching. It was about two inches wide and had decorative metal strips wound around the center of it that made it look very much like the wide bracelets and neck cuffs worn by members of several African tribes.

Sybil's bracelet fit snugly on her wrist just above the wrist bone. There was no visible closing; it almost seemed like it was attached to her arm and, as far as anyone knew, she never took it off.

This unique bracelet added to the mystery of Sybil. It was assuredly noticed by everyone but never mentioned or questioned as to where she got it, why she wore it, or whether or not she ever removed it.

After things were set up for the Garden Club's affair, Sybil got into her car and headed into town where she planned to meet Pottsy for a quiet, relaxing dinner. As she drove, she went over all the arrangements in her head and smiled, realizing it was definitely going to be perfect.

Absorbed in her thoughts, Sybil failed to notice the speeding car and was surprised when she felt the impact.

The door on the driver's side was the main point of impact, and the crushed metal was holding Sybil tightly, trapping her arm between the door and the seat. They had to use cutters to remove the door and free her from the wreckage. She moaned and then cried out in pain as the door moved, and her arm fell free. She couldn't help the scream that filled the car and brought tears to the eyes of onlookers.

Medics worked quickly to get Sybil onto the waiting stretcher, one taking vitals as another inserted and started an IV, being careful not to touch the injured arm as they moved her into the ambulance.

Emergency room doctors quickly accessed her condition, finding that besides the broken and crushed arm, she only had a few bruises and two small lacerations. They quickly agreed that Sybil's bracelet would have to be cut off so that the arm wounds could be addressed and began working even as Sybil cried and pleaded with them not to remove her bracelet. Her tears and pleas were heart-wrenching but to no effect as doctors carefully began to cut the metal.

Finally the wide band was open and as the doctor began to peel it back, Sybil whispered, "No, No, No, please No." Then she passed out.

"What the hell?" As these words exploded from the doctor's mouth, others people in the room saw the reason...

Beneath the wide cuff bracelet was another sort of bracelet... a handcuff with two links of chain still attached.

Mama's Surprise

When I answered the ringing doorbell, the FedEx man said, "Is your father here?"

I almost giggled because no one I knew said "father" anymore. It was either dad, pops or something else equally casual.

I answered that, "No, he's not here but my mama is."

"OK," he said. "She can sign for the package."

Mama signed, then took the small box he held out to her.

Tearing open the package, she was shocked to see a beautiful, sparkling diamond pendant. She gasped in delight.

There was a note attached that read, "My dearest darling, you are the sparkle in my eye. Someday I'll be free and we'll be together. Love always, Dan."

Mama's delight quickly turned to shock and then to anger as she realized that the package had mistakenly been delivered to the address of the sender and not to the woman whose name appeared on the shipping label.

A Special Day

Sunlight streamed through open curtains, the brightness waking her. Finally, the day had come, it was the ninth of June and she had to get up and get ready.

After dressing and combing her hair, she pulled on her best sweater, tied her sneakers and went to join her family. The kitchen was a busy, noisy place with everyone hurrying around, getting ready to go off and do whatever it was they did every day.

Talking over each other, plans for the day were made and soon, everyone was saying goodbye and rushing out the door. She was alone. Tears threatened as she stood there, wishing that they had remembered this was a special day.

She would just have to go alone. It seemed like a good idea, at least if she didn't think too long or too hard about it. Clutching her purse, she went out the door, careful to lock it behind her. The downtown bus picked her up at the corner and her journey began.

After getting off the bus, she walked three blocks to Sycamore Street and stood on the curb, waiting for the walk light to flash. There were lots of people around her, pushing, shoving and moving her closer to the edge of the curb. She was feeling a little tired and, to tell the truth, this was all a little frightening.

She felt a touch on her arm and warily pulled her purse closer. The voice in her ear was familiar and she felt relief as she looked up at her son. "Mom, I'm sorry I forgot that today was special for you; we'll go the rest of the way together.

She leaned closer to him as they stepped off the curb and, with the crowd all around them, crossed the street, turned left and continued toward their destination, a small church that sat on the next corner. She stopped at the foot of the steps and tears shimmered in her eyes despite her tremulous smile. Then, taking a deep breath, she put her foot on the first step and began the short climb.

The years dropped away as they entered the cool dimness of the church and walked slowly down the aisle toward the altar where sixty three years ago she had married the man she loved. Clutching her son's arm, she whispered, "This is where I feel closest to him... right here where we stood and said our vows. Oh, how we loved each other that day and every day of our time together. And then, years later, I said my goodbye and kissed his cheek for the last time here in this church."

She murmured a prayer, crossed herself and then, turning slowly, said, "Take me home now. I'm a little tired."

Bad Way to Start the Day

The bank teller looked at my check and then with an embarrassed smile said, "I just have to get this approved."

A few minutes later, she emerged from the manager's office and said that he would like to speak to me.

"I'm sorry, Mrs. Jones but we can't cash this check."

Stunned by his words, I could only sit there with my mouth open.

"But my check book shows there is over $5,000 in my account, why can't you cash my check?"

"The money is gone... all gone. Your husband withdrew it yesterday."

Then it hit me... John had not gone on a weeklong business trip... he had left me! He was gone and with him all the money in our account.

Seeking a Suitable Solution

Well, this is certainly a dilemma. The judge ordered me to pay alimony to that jerk I was married to! Alimony money that he'll only blow on booze, women of very questionable repute and sleazy motels – my money!

I sipped my wine and tried to change my line of thought to something more pleasant but… nothing came to mind except that maybe I should have hired some thug to put a bullet through his knee as a warning when he left me and became increasingly annoying with his constant phone calls and pleas for one more chance". Ha! Like that was even an option.

Anyway, the sob story he told in court, mostly all lies by the way, convinced the judge to grant him $100 a week.

So here I am now, mad as hell but stuck with paying it. So the elephant in the room has won but, you know what, maybe it's worth $100 a week to have a life again.

The Dance

The dress, with its beautifully draped neckline and fitted waist, was the prettiest I'd ever seen. It was a delicious soft rose in color and the skirt swished softly around my legs as I walked across the floor, making me feel feminine and glowing.

I saw him standing there by the bar, handsome in his tux, a smile on his face as he held his arms open to me.

The music was soft jazz and sent out a clear invitation to dance to its romantic beat. His arms closed about me as we began to move; there was no need for words. I felt as if we were the only two people on earth at that moment.

I closed my eyes and breathed in his scent, so familiar and so loved. He held me close and I could feel his breath on my cheek and in my ear, making me shiver with pleasure. I was lost.

Then, I opened my eyes and realized I was crying. Why? Where had the moment gone?

Then I knew…

The dream had been so real and so beautiful.

Taking A Risk

He sat down beside her and took her hand. She looked down, not willing to meet his eyes and see the disappointment she was sure he felt.

"Come on, just try it once, I promise it won't be as bad as you think. It's like riding a bicycle, once you've done it, you never forget how."

Trying to lift her mood, he laughed as she spoke.

"I just don't think I can... it's been so long."

Rubbing the back of her hand, he implored, "Just try it with me, and if you feel uncomfortable or if anything hurts, we'll stop."

"It's scary after all this time. I do want to do it with you, but I just don't know if I can."

They just sat quietly for a few minutes; he continued to stroke her hand as she looked down with a worried frown on her face.

Then her frown disappeared and, turning her head to look at him, she saw the longing in his eyes. He had promised her a special afternoon...

Gathering her courage, she said, "OK, let's do it!"

With a smile as wide as the Ohio River, he helped her to her feet and then, as the music began again, he took her hand, and they moved onto the polished floor of the skating rink and blended into the slow-moving skaters gliding not so smoothly along the rail.

Disaster Journal
(Daily Log Entries, December 10 & 11, 1982)

11:30 PM – December 10, 1982

On the 11:00 news tonight, Nick Clooney reported that nuclear war is imminent. He emphasized that those who have prepared for this "long shot" possibility by building nuclear bomb shelters make final preparation for the stay in these shelters. We must now go over the list of supplies in our shelter and make certain that all is ready. We have until 10:00 AM tomorrow.

6:00 AM – December 11, 1982

We have worked all night to get everything set for our move into the shelter. I'm really scared but can't let Al know. Tonight as we checked supplies, carried in fresh water and certain medical needs, we've gone over the names and lives of the people who live here in the building with us. Some of them will be sharing our lives for the duration of our stay in the shelter and will be sharing the problems and hard work involved in staying alive after we emerge into whatever is left of the world that we know. It's going to be tough leaving the rest of our friends behind, but I feel they all understand why we made the choices we did.

We have to look ahead and plan even now as we go into the shelter.

7:00 AM – December 11, 1982

The morning news on every station warns that time is not to be wasted. The whole city is frantic. Boy, it seems strange to write these notes which are the beginning of a log of a period in my life that I certainly had thought was not ever likely to occur. As I write now, I realize that my normal morning routine is still guiding me. I put on the teakettle, measured out instant coffee crystals in my favorite cup, listened for the whistle then reached behind me to turn off the burner when the kettle sang. Well, now we have to get everybody together and ready to go to the shelter. They have had several hours to get their personal matters resolved and should be all set. It's going to seem funny not to sit here every morning, having my coffee and watching squirrels and birds play in the trees. This last hour has been spent putting some personal belongings in the shelter and in saying goodbyes and words of comfort to other friends and neighbors. Some of them we'll see again and some of them will not survive this dreadful time. Now everyone seems fairly well prepared for this moment, not a lot of panic but a lot of sadness.

9:30 AM – December 11, 1982

We're all in the shelter now and the doors are sealed. Everyone has brought necessities and a few personal things.

We each have our allocated space that we will use for personal items. We have checked all facilities and equipment and everything is fine. Everyone is getting settled in. I've convinced Al to lie down and rest a while. This is going to take some getting used to. I've had to really work on my claustrophobia. Of course, as long as I can feel the movement of air in the shelter, I'm o.k.

I'm going to keep this log on a daily basis while we're here. I'll just try to describe everyone here in the shelter. I'll also explain why each one was selected.

Al and I have looked carefully at the possibility that our group will be all alone when we emerge and will need to have talent to begin a new life from scratch. Even though he has a heart condition, with a good supply of his medication here and with the amount of rest he'll be able to get, he should be able to carry his part of the load while we are living in the shelter. He'll be important to us after we come out again too.

Oh God! It's finally going to hit me; the awful finality of what is happening to us! What will become of all the trees, the birds and flowers? Oh, I miss my beautiful garden and lawn, my house with its sunny corners and happy secrets. Will we ever survive and smell the wonderful scent of rain and wet grass again? Oh God, help me through this, keep me strong for the sake of all of us. Help me!

I got my crying over and nobody knows about it. Everything seems better now. We've just assembled in the center of our shelter and discussed how we'll handle our work assignments and also how we'll handle any problems or emergency. Everybody understands the importance of our pulling together and our getting along.

Oh, yes, I had started to list everybody who is here with us and I'll get to that now before I get sidetracked again. First of all, we needed a leader, someone to pull us together both here and later when we go outside. Harry was chosen to fit this role. He is 50 years old, a professor of American History and well-versed in the political structure of our country.

Harry is extremely well organized, personable and a natural leader. Highly respected by all of us and trusted, he'll be our stabilizer. In addition, his knowledge of history will be invaluable when we come out and get our new towns and neighborhoods established.

Next, we have Barry. He is a bio-chemist who is 40 years old and has a drinking problem. We've talked about the problem, and Barry has been attending AA meetings over the past month. He is trying to beat this problem and we'll help him through this withdrawal period in every way we can. He has some medication which will help, but more than that, he's important here and he knows how much we all need his skills and expertise in the chemical field. We are counting on his strength and total commitment to our survival.

John is 22 years old and an Olympic athlete. We need his strength and stamina. He is young and virile and will be able to father many children when we are ready to repopulate our world. He is friendly, open and very important to us for many reasons.

Nancy is 31 years old and has varied skills. She is a bookkeeper and will be valuable as a teacher to our young ones in the future. For now, she'll be able to assist in a number of ways; she will keep track of our supplies on a daily basis and will keep all records of our stay here. (This log is for my own therapy as well as a means of recording things as I see them.)

Finally we have Barbara, who is 16 years old and is now three months pregnant. While her I.Q has been questioned by some, she is a warm, outgoing, neat and hardworking young lady. Her life has not been the easiest, so she has learned how to handle the waiting and disappointments that sometimes come along. She is going to give birth about the time we are ready to go outside gain. This will be our baby, our 'new beginning'. Barbara will be able to produce children and will be a good mother to her family. She will be a joy to all of us.

Each of these people will contribute to our daily routine. We'll read, exercise, plan for the future, and try to develop and hone all our senses and skills to the maximum. It'll be tough; days will be long and, at times, may seem unbearable; but with life as the prize, we can and will all make it.

<u>9:30 PM – December 11, 1982</u>

We've now been here for 12 hours. I don't know what's going on outside. This first day has gone pretty good. I'm sure everyone here has had their private time today with

53

some tears and doubts. We'll mark off the days on our calendar and be thankful we're safe and warm with all the ingredients here to plan and implement a new way of life when the time comes.

This log book will be my best friend and confidant as the days pass. There will be some tear stains I'm sure, but there will also be some smiles reflected in my recording the daily life here. For this, the end of my first day in the shelter, I'll close my entry by saying goodnight and goodbye. Tomorrow brings a new day.

Personal Essays
and
Other True Stories

How the Dictionary Changed My Life

He expected everyone, even his employees, to call him Bill. When I met him, he was probably around 60 years old. Bill and his wife Alice, a tall slender, no-nonsense kind of woman with definite opinions about practically everything, owned an auto parts store in Hammond, Indiana. Like Alice, Bill was tall but he didn't have the same slender build that she had. He was an attractive man despite the few extra pounds around his middle. He generally had a smile on his face, and he loved to talk.

Bill was retired so he came to the store for some period of time each day. He usually came in the late morning and stayed till around 3 o'clock. While there, he could be found greeting customers and chatting with them as they waited for their orders to be written up or sometimes he would walk up and down the aisles, straightening shelves or helping someone fill outside orders that the salesmen would later deliver. All the employees liked him, and he was careful to never interfere with their work or to make them feel that he was checking on them. Everyone knew that he was just generally keeping busy while at the same time being friendly and social.

Alice was the brains of the operation. She did all of the bookkeeping and pretty much ran the business. She was also well-liked by the employees, but she was strict and, being German, very outspoken, so even though they liked her, they respected her role as the boss. Both Alice and Mary Ann, the lady who worked in the office with her, were kind to me and I learned a lot from them. Although they were much older, they were friendly and in reality, they were motherly to me. They worked hard and even though they were friendly with each other, they didn't spend a lot of time gabbing.

Alice and Mary Ann worked in a glass-enclosed office that opened to the area where I sat. My desk had a glass half partition separating it from the store's main area. The store manager, Gordon also had a desk in that area and the perpetual inventory system was also set up there. I was the cashier and I maintained the inventory cards as well as tallying sales receipts and processing some billing.

I was 20 years old, not even old enough to vote when I went to work for them. I don't remember how I got the job and don't remember interviewing for it, but I'll never forget the people I worked with there. I worked there for about seven years then quit to move to Kentucky. However, after staying in Kentucky for a couple of months, we moved back to Hammond and I was able to get my job back. I worked there another couple of years, leaving only for a better job.

I had to work every other Saturday from 8AM to noon. Those days turned out to be some of the best in my life.

The store generally wasn't as busy on Saturday. Neither Alice, Mary Ann nor Gordon, the store manager worked on Saturdays. Hence, it was usually just Bill and me other than the two or three counter employees and one person in the machine shop.

Since the store wasn't very busy on Saturday mornings, Bill and I would sit in my area and talk. As I mentioned before, Bill loved to talk; he had been in the Navy for several years and had been practically everywhere. He had a rooster tattooed on his instep, the left one I think, and he told me that getting a rooster tattoo was a ritual that sailors went through when they crossed the equator; he also told me that he had crossed the equator more than once. You can imagine how impressed I was hearing all of this. I had never known anyone who had done those exciting things.

I was enthralled with the stories Bill told and I asked a lot of questions. Bill came up with the game for us to play on Saturday mornings that went like this… Bill would open the dictionary to a random page, choose a word and then give me that word to define and spell. We would go through this exercise all morning when I wasn't busy at the cash register.

I was amazed and very pleased with how well I did with the words he gave me. Sometimes, if it was a totally new word to me, he would give me the definition and then ask me to use the word in a sentence. We had several wonderful conversations regarding this exercise, a particular word, or even the spelling of it. Little did I realize then what a valuable learning experience our game provided to me.

I can still see Bill even now… sitting at Gordon's desk, feet propped up on an open drawer, and leaning back in his chair with the dictionary open in his hands. Bill always wore a hat and placed it on his head in a manner that hid the top of his right ear. I had noticed that Bill also had a bandage on the top of that ear, but I hadn't asked about it because I didn't feel like it was appropriate for me to do so. Later on, I found that the reason for his wearing the hat and hiding that ear was because he had had cancer on that ear a few years prior and had had some surgery that took the top of his ear off. Then after a few years, the cancer had come back, and he was adamant about not seeing a doctor or doing anything to try to help it. So over time, the cancer had gotten pretty bad and, at that point, it was just a large, very unsightly, bloody, scabby-looking thing and that's why he kept it covered. While of course, nobody ever asked about it or said anything about it, we did notice that over the years, Bill kept it covered more and more; the bandage grew to a size that covered the whole ear and sometimes the bandage would be bloody looking. Even though he tried to hide it with his hat, it had become very apparent that the ear was getting worse.

While all this was going on with Bill's ear, Alice was diagnosed with breast cancer. She had a mastectomy; I believe it was just one side, not both. That was sometime in the early sixties and, at that time; they had not performed mastectomies all that often. This was a very difficult time for Alice. Taking care of the business and undergoing her rehabilitation after the loss of her breast and worrying about Bill all the time was very telling on her and she became rather gaunt and quieter than usual, but she never let on that it was difficult for her.

Finally, one morning, Alice didn't come to work and instead called Mary Ann to say that during the night, Bill's ear had literally exploded. He had hemorrhaged so badly that they had blood everywhere and of course, she had taken him to a hospital. At the hospital, after they stopped the hemorrhaging, the doctor tried to address the severity of the cancer with Bill and Alice and again suggested that surgery could possibly delay the inevitable although the cancer had gone into the brain and that was what caused the severe hemorrhaging. But, again, Bill was just not having them do anything to it, although he understood what the outcome would be and that his remaining time was limited. But he again said no, he did not want to have any surgery, and he accepted his fate.

Bill did live several months after that, but he didn't come into the office anymore. Alice altered her regular work schedule so that she was home with Bill several hours a day. She did everything she could to take care of Bill, the business and the store's employees. She was a hard-working woman, a wonderful woman, actually.

I also learned a lot from Alice. I learned a lot about work ethics and about being steady. I learned about doing what you said you would do and about being responsible. And one time, when I had to go to her house to take some work over to her, I entered her home to the smell of apples. She was sitting in a sunroom with the sunlight streaming in the window, across her desk and everything shone like new. It smelled so clean and fresh and that smell of apples just filled me with the most wonderful feelings! I've never forgotten that moment when I walked into Alice's house and witnessed the sunlight streaming into the room, and the smell of those apples and furniture polish filled me, and I thought to myself, "This is the way rich people live and I want to live like this, with the smell of apples always with me."

In all the years I've worked, I've thought of Bill and Alice so many times, and I thought about the wonderful things they gave to me, a young woman just starting her work life, through their time, their attention, and their teachings, and I've tried to do the same thing for others around me.

God Bless people like Bill and Alice.

Birthdays are Special

Yesterday was my birthday.

The night before my big day, I started feeling like the next day was a milestone of some sort and really started to feel a little unsettled about the coming birthday. Oh sure, I was going to be another year older, but up until a few years ago, that hadn't bothered me. But, as my Auntie Rene used to say, "I have more years behind me that I have in front." That bothers me. Just thinking about that truth certainly brings mortality into play.

As I sat there mulling over what my birthday might actually mean and what changes might occur as a result of being a year older, I realized that I was feeling disheartened by the thought that I might change. Change? How?

Would I no longer laugh? Would reading cease to captivate me for hours on end? Would the sweet aroma that comes from my favorite coffeehouse fail to entice me? Would the life wrinkles on my face have changed and grown more prominent? Would I still love anything with spinach in it? Would I become a different me? Stop it! I know that I am being morose and silly thinking like this.

But I know I will have to acknowledge that I am another year older every time I have to provide my birthdate or see it in writing on a document. And along with that acknowledgment, I will also have to admit that my time on earth is growing shorter, and that's what I'm really concerned about.

You see, I don't feel my age. I feel the same as I did when I was 50. I feel energized by the thought of what life holds for me; I am excited about learning new things, about having new experiences, about having another day to try to make life better for someone around me. Every day I find joy in watching the red birds flit about in the trees behind my condo. I am always stunned by the beauty of the clouds, and I'm captivated by the flowers that pop up on hillsides, in pots and gardens. I am thankful for the family and friends who call or email to chat or to make plans for some event. I am forever grateful to our loving God for the blessings I receive daily.

When I woke up on the morning of my birthday, I said a quick prayer of thanks for being given another day, a day that was special, my own day. I realized that my fears and concerns were gone and I felt happy! I also realized that I had been given the wonderful gift of more time in this life. And I knew that being a year older did not change me in the ways I had feared but that I was still the same person I had been the day before. I would still laugh, still find joy in the day, love food and enjoy talking with people around me. I would still be the curious sort that I've always been, and I would still not like housework!

My birthday turned out to be an exceptional day. I had an appointment with my cardiologist and both the receptionist and the doctor wished me a happy birthday. The doctor even apologized for having booked my appointment on my birthday.

Last evening, I went to an event where I was with a group of people who all wished me a happy birthday and then insisted that I take all the leftover desserts home with me because it was my birthday. Since I love sweets, that was a great ending to a fun and noisy evening where music and friends were the main features.

So now I am a year older... so what?

My Chevy and Me

I can't recall exactly when, or under what circumstances I got my first car, but I do recall clearly that it was a 1963 baby blue Chevy BelAir. I probably remember it so vividly because it was the very first time I had a car that was all mine.

It was probably somewhere around the end of 1967 or early 1968 that I got the car. At that time, there were lots of things going on in my life, and those events probably wiped out details about the car.

In September 1969, my husband and I were divorced. Early the next year, I drove my Chevy to Ft. Wayne, Indiana, stayed with my brother's family for a couple of weeks, and then found a job and a small furnished apartment. I quickly realized that my paycheck would not stretch to cover rent, insurance, food, etc., so I quit that job and went back to Kentucky to stay with my parents.

Then something exciting happened! I had a call from Blount Brothers, the construction company I had previously worked for, and they asked me to go to another job with them. The job was in Cincinnati, Ohio. Of course I said YES to this opportunity.

Early in the morning of April 23, 1970, I left my mother's house in Western Kentucky and began my first adventure alone. At that time, I knew nothing about Cincinnati, not even where it was located; I didn't even know that Ohio was just across the river from Kentucky.

I had celebrated my 34th birthday just days before this adventure began.

In preparation for the trip, I had gotten my Chevy BelAir serviced, loaded a few necessities in the back seat along with my clothes and I had gotten directions that would take me to Cincinnati and to the Carousel Inn, where my company was housing employees of the project until offices were ready to occupy.

Waving goodbye to my parents, I pulled out onto the road and I began the 300-mile trip that would change my life by giving me a chance to start anew as a single, independent woman. The drive was uneventful. I had never taken a trip alone before and I had never driven on an expressway. I had never even thought about how it would be to drive in a large city. Everything was totally new, and I considered it an adventure.

I had blonde hair that was teased in a 1970's style that was big and heavily sprayed; my Chevy was baby blue, and I couldn't remember which hand signal meant a right turn and which meant left. So when I needed to signal a turn, I would just put my arm out the window and wiggle it around, figuring other drivers would see it and know that I was going to do something. After all, I was a blonde in a baby blue car with Kentucky license plates, so any odd behaviors could be attributed to those conditions. It must have worked because I made the drive without anyone yelling at me, giving me dirty looks, or a one-finger salute. Maybe that's because I drove the speed limit and stayed in the slow lane unless forced to move over to pass someone slower than me.

I felt free and was very excited about the opportunity facing me.

It was early afternoon when I rounded the curve at the spot known locally as "the cut in the hill" and there before me, the city of Cincinnati stood, stately and large. I was absolutely awestruck and exclaimed, "Oh, how beautiful!" This incredible city was to be my new home, and I was amazed at the beauty around me. Today, almost fifty years later, I am still struck by the view when I round that curve and see the panorama that is Cincinnati and Northern Kentucky glistening in the sunlight or lighted brightly at night.

The view impressed me in 1970 and will continue to do so. I have blossomed and grown in this city, made great friends and had a truly rewarding career. Most importantly, I met the love of my life in this city and, even though I moved to Houston, Texas for a short while in 1976, I couldn't wait to get back to my adopted city. Leaving my Kentucky roots and coming to Cincinnati was the right move for me in 1970 and over the years, I've grown into a true Cincinnatian. I was definitely impressed that long-ago day, and that feeling has never changed.

Animal Kingdom

A crazy, acrobatic chipmunk somehow got on top of the bird feeder and proceeded to gobble down the new Cranberry Nut feed cylinder I'd just put out.

I quickly opened the door to yell at him, and that set off the security alarm, which I hadn't yet turned off. OOPS!

I scared him away three times altogether. By then, he had eaten it all, and I was still trying to figure out how to get him to leave.

Obviously, it had become a battle of wits, and I'm pretty sure that he won!

A Scary Storm

Early on the morning of January 26, 1967 it began snowing. Even though the forecast was for a heavy accumulation of four inches or more with a high temperature in the lower 30's and winds fifteen to twenty-five mph, I went to work as usual. I worked for the Mattress Workers Union Local #454 in Munster, Indiana which was several miles from where I lived.

By mid-morning, another forecast was issued saying that an additional four to eight inches of snow was expected with steady winds of twenty-five to thirty-five mph.

By noon eight inches had accumulated, and businesses were sending employees home. It was getting very windy, and the snow was beginning to drift; it was really piling up fast. I heard on the radio that buses had stopped running and major streets were being closed. People were being warned not to get out but to stay in their homes or business. I wanted to get home.

When I got to the parking lot, I found that snow was already up over the bottom of my car door, and I couldn't get the door open. I went into the meat store next door to see if one of the men there could help me get my car out. They told me that I shouldn't even think about trying to get home. The brothers who owned the store, along with Anna, the wife of one of them, were planning to stay all night in the store; they said I should stay there with them so I would be safe. I didn't want to do that, I wanted to get home. I thought my family would be worried about me. I couldn't even contact anyone at home because the phones were also out by that time.

It was only mid-afternoon, but it looked like it was dusk. The storm was really getting bad, and it was expected to get worse. By this time, we had heard the expressways going in and out of Chicago had been closed and that tractor-trailer trucks, as well as cars, were stranded all along the road. People that were stranded were being warned not to get out of their cars to try to get help.

One of the stranded trucks belonged to the meat store. They decided to take one of their work vans and try to get to the stranded truck so they could off-load the expensive load of meat and try to get it, and the driver, back to the store safely. When I asked if I could ride with them, they tried to convince me to stay there in the store where I would be safe and warm, but when they realized I was determined to get home, they said I could ride with them since they would be passing an exit that would get me close to the neighborhood where I lived.

They loaded all kinds of tools, chains, blankets, sand, food and water into the van, and we left the store. Progress was very slow; cars were abandoned everywhere; traffic lights were not working, and it was often difficult to determine just where the street was. It was slow and treacherous. Some three hours later, we had finally made it the few miles from the store onto the expressway. The snow was blowing and swirling so hard that it was extremely difficult to see. It was scary.

After driving for a long time, the van came to a stop. One of the brothers told me that I could get home by going up the ramp where we were stopped. He also said they didn't think I should try it, but they understood my determination to get home. I got out of the van into a thick blanket of snow and a wind that was, by that time, howling.

I was wearing a three-quarter-length coat which was a leopard print. It was thick and furry and quite warm. I hadn't worn anything on my head that day, but I did have a neck scarf which I tied around my head as I headed out into the blowing snow. My boots were dress boots that came up just below the knees; fortunately they were pretty low-heeled so I could walk in them fairly well. I was not wearing slacks or tights, only nylon stockings. I was not dressed for this kind of weather but... I ducked my head into the wind and started walking.

By this time, it was quite dark. The snow made it very hard to see and the wind was so cold it was hard to breathe. Several vehicles had pulled over and now sat, covered with snow, looking deserted. Many of them had their motors running, so I assumed that people were in them. Several times I stopped behind a vehicle to try to get warm and to get my breath.

Finally, before I was even up to the top of the ramp, I was so cold I had to stop. There was a big semi sitting there with its motor running; I ducked behind it and stood there, warming my hands in the heat from the truck's exhaust. I was so terribly cold!

I knew that I needed to thaw out before I could go further. I tapped on the window and when a man opened it, I asked if I could get in to get warm. He opened the passenger side door and I got into the warm cab. At this point I wasn't even thinking of my safety; I was just too cold and too tired.

The trucker who had opened his door to me was a middle-aged man. He was very kind and cautioned me about getting into cars or trucks with strangers even in this situation; he said there were people who would take advantage of a situation. He turned his truck heater on full force and rubbed my hands to get feeling back into them. I was so grateful for his kindness.

After a while I felt warmer, so I thanked him for his kindness, got out of the truck and again headed toward home. It was dark by that time; the snow was even heavier and the wind was fierce. The scarf on my head and my gloves did little to keep me warm even though I walked with my head down and my hands in my pockets. I could hardly get through the deep snow and within minutes, I was once again freezing. I prayed.

Then, after what seemed a long time, I saw a street light ahead, glowing yellow through the swirling snow, leaving a bright circle of welcome around it. I finally made it up to the street and saw that it was mine. I felt so happy thinking I had almost made it home. The snow was so deep by then that I couldn't lift my feet high enough to make a step but had to drag them forward. It was even slower going than before. It was also getting colder by the minute, and I was exhausted!

I could see lights in the houses as I slogged through the snow, down what appeared to be the middle of the street, as I tried to get home. Finally, I saw the lights of my mother-in-law's house, which was a couple of houses up the street from ours. I turned into her yard, making my way toward the house, and took every last bit of my energy just trying to get to the door. When I was about halfway from the street to the house, I could see them all sitting at the kitchen table and knew I was within reach of warmth and safety. Then I fell.

The snow was up to my knees, and I just couldn't go any further. I tried to get up but couldn't. I started yelling "HELP, HELP" as loud as I could, although I knew the howling wind would make it difficult for anyone to hear me. I was desperate and thought I had failed when no one came outside. At that point, I thought my efforts had been in vain and they would find me there in the yard when morning came, frozen and dead.

Then I saw my mother-in-law open the kitchen door and look out toward the street. I yelled again, "HELP, HELP." She stood there for a minute, her head cocked toward the wind, before turning back into the house. I thought surely she hadn't heard my desperate cry for help. And then the door opened again, and I saw my husband and his step-father moving cautiously away from the house and toward where I sat, half-buried, in the snow.

They helped me into the house and everyone gathered around me, happy to see me. When they unzipped one of my boots and started to pull it off, my stocking came stretching out as the boot was pulled off; my boot was packed with snow and the stocking had frozen to the boot.

I was colder than I would have imagined anyone could possibly be. They got me out of my wet clothes, wrapped me in warm blankets, dried my hair which was dripping as it thawed, put my feet in hot water and gave me some soup. It took a long time, but I finally warmed up enough to tell them my story about how I had gotten home. It had taken me six to seven hours to get there but I had made it. I was so thankful.

It continued to snow for the next couple of days and the blizzard went down in the records as one of the three worst ever in the Chicago area. Twenty-three inches of snow fell that day and more fell in the next couple of days. There were drifts up to six feet in many places and some drifts of eight-ten feet were reported. It took several days to get the stranded cars and trucks cleared off the roads and interstates. There were also some fatalities from the storm; I'm happy that I wasn't one of them, although at times that cold night, I was sure I would be.

My Interesting Drive-Thru Experience

On Monday of last week, I called Brooke, my Personal Banker at Wes Banco.

"Hi, Brooke,"

"Hi, how are things going for you? Everything O.K. with your account?"

"Yeah, things are going fine, no problems. I just wanted to tell you that I'm getting a new car and selling my old one, so I need to get the title notarized. Can you do that for me?"

"Oh yeah, I can do that, but you'll have to come to the drive-thru window since the bank is closed to the public because of the virus."

"O.K., if everything goes according to plan, my grandson will fly to Chicago on Tuesday morning, pick up my new car and drive it back to Cincinnati for me. I have notified the buyer that if all goes well, he can pick up my old car on Wednesday or any time afterward."

The plan went well, and my new car did indeed arrive in Cincinnati on Tuesday afternoon. I called Stacy, the buyer, and he told me he would pick up the car on Wednesday after he got off work. So, on Wednesday afternoon, I headed to the bank with the title in hand. That's when the fun started!

When I pulled into the parking lot, I realized that I didn't know where the drive-thru was. I had previously only used the ATM lane, so I pulled in there to see if that was also the drive-thru. Nope, I was only looking at the

ATM, which wanted my card to make any transaction. I didn't want to do that.

I sat there in my car, wondering how in the heck I could get this title notarized if I couldn't get in touch with someone inside the bank. Then I noticed a large glass window on the same wall as the ATM and I thought, "Ah ha, I can just tap on the window and get the attention of someone inside."

So I got out of my car and walked up to the window. I could see two tellers and the bank manager inside. Still, despite my knocking on the window, they didn't acknowledge my presence, so then I started waving my arms and the manager saw me standing there.

She came to the window, laughing and saying something but I couldn't hear her. I said, "I can't hear you." But I continued to stand there at the window and watched her mouth move as she was trying to talk to me. She pointed to something behind me. I turned and then walked over to another lane where I saw a canister in a glass tube and buttons beside it that would allow me to send the canister to her. There was a speaker beside the buttons and I could hear her just fine. I realized that I had located the drive-thru.

So I told her what I needed. I asked her where I should sign the title, she looked puzzled, so I walked over to the big window and held the title up to the glass. (Now someone watching this play out might have thought I was some dumb criminal trying to hold up the bank in the drive-thru!)

I told her that I had never been through a drive-thru before and that I needed training. She laughed and said,

"Just send it in, and I'll fill out my part and put an X where you need to sign."

In the meantime, I asked if I needed to move my car over to the drive-thru lane and she said, "Yes, that's a good idea, I don't want you to get hurt when the canister comes flying back." Not being able to make the sharp turn necessary to move to the next lane, I drove out through the parking lot and pulled into the lane just like I knew what I was doing.

I pulled the canister out of its resting place. "How do I get this thing open?"

Before she could answer, I realized that by turning it sideways, there was an opening I could access by flipping the lid. Feeling proud, I put the title inside, inserted the canister into the tube and pressed the button that said, 'Send Canister'. There was loud WHOOSHING noise that caused me to jump back and let out a yelp.

She filled out her part, asking me questions about who was buying it, the mileage and how much he was paying for the car. She needed to see my driver's license and sent the tube back so I could send it in to her. Then she returned the title for my signature. Finally, I had the signed and notarized title and my driver's license back in my possession. But I have to admit that I jumped back every time that canister went up or down.

The buyer picked up my car on Wednesday afternoon and gave me a cashier's check in payment.

On Thursday afternoon, I went back to WesBanco to deposit the check. Feeling pretty superior in my drive-thru knowledge and experience, I confidently pulled into the drive-thru lane and saw Brooke standing at the window waiting for me. "Hi Brooke, I was here yesterday and Michelle notarized the title for me and now I need to deposit the check."

With a big smile on her face, Brook replied, "Yes, I heard about your visit yesterday."

So the moral of this story is… Don't believe that old saying about not being able to teach an old dog new tricks… I can tell you first-hand that sometimes "an old dog needs to learn a new trick!"

The Gray House

Strange as it may seem, this story, about a house, is told here just as it was revealed to me by the house itself.

I first noticed the house a few years ago when a woman named Dottie joined 'The Laid Back Ladies', a chapter of the then-popular Red Hat Society that I had started a couple of years previously.

When we first met, Dottie and I had discovered that we lived fairly close together and that I frequently passed her house on my way home. So, one day at our monthly Red Hat luncheon, Dottie asked if I could give her a ride home that day. Of course, I said yes.

She pointed to a rather smallish white 2-story house that sat just barely off the street, surrounded by woods that seemed to be closing in on the house. It was perched on a hillside lot with the garage at street level and the house built into the sloping terrain. It sat there pretty nicely but not in a spot that added any appeal to the house.

Dottie, who was 74 at the time, was a newlywed and the couple had bought this odd little house to begin their life together.

There wasn't much yard as a semi-circular drive took up the space where a lawn would have been; the street dropped down and then disappeared into a sharp curve. I realized that the half-circle drive was necessary since there was no safe way to enter or exit from the street.

About a year later, Dottie and her new husband had to move from the house to a condo for health reasons and the house sat with only a realtor's sign to pull attention to it. It had a sad and lonely look as weeds grew closer to the house. When fall arrived, the falling leaves built up in layers or were blown into piles before the wind eventually moved them into the woods. Then one day the next spring, I saw a truck in the drive and the garage door stood open. A couple of days later, a SOLD sign appeared in the yard.

I often passed the house and silently cheered on the men who soon began working around the house. It became evident that some extensive changes and remodeling were planned. A window was added to the side of the garage, adding interest to the area surrounding the front door.

The existing window in the front of the house became a large bay window and an outside stairway to the second floor soon climbed up the side of the house that sloped toward the woods. Work proceeded slowly as all the work was being done by a couple of young men who looked to be in their 30s.

They did beautiful work and cleaned up their mess when they finished each day. Soon the house had a new roof, a new garage door, and some decorative trim that showed off the fresh coat of gray and white paint. This new color scheme was striking, and I found myself purposely passing that way just to see their progress.

Sometime later in the summer, a young couple with two children moved into the house. The windows sparkled, flower pots appeared, and the little house practically glowed. Finishing work continued, each change making the house more attractive. It now seemed to nestle into the curving drive, and it blended beautifully into the wooded area that accentuated the sloping lot. The house and its surroundings now seemed to be one unit, no longer pulled apart but blended.

The big bay window looked into what was obviously a small dining room and on dreary days, I would often see the two little kids working on projects at the table. Although I never saw their mother, I knew she must be a good one.

One day that summer, I saw the two little ones, probably about 3 and 4 years old at the time, standing there, looking out the window, both stark naked! They were laughing as their little hands patted the window. You could see the joy on their faces. I'm sure their mother was mortified when she found them there in the window and realized that people passing by had seen this exhibition. Poor mama!

That house just got better and better as months went by. The young couple put in so much love and labor and I'm sure they treasured their little gray and white house. It looked like a much-loved home.

I moved away from the area a year ago and seldom drove past the house anymore. Then, one day recently, I did drive by and almost drove off the road when I saw the charred roof with a large gaping hole beside the large chimney. Parts of the house were hanging, damaged by the fire that evidently ravished this beautiful little house. I was shocked and felt very sad. I do hope no one was injured in the fire that had consumed the house.

Since that time, I've seen a large sign in the yard that thanked the neighbors and the community for their support, love, and generosity. I am positive that this young couple, like the Phoenix, will rise and that where once a lovely and much-loved home stood, there will be another that will be loved even more. Young couples are just that passionate about life!

And frankly, who would have ever thought that a house could tell such a story of commitment, love, and family? Well, this little gray and white house certainly did!

Where Did Thanksgiving Go?

A couple of weeks ago, when the calendar turned over to December, it occurred to me that the everyday pace of life had escalated. Well, now that I think about it, the pace actually had quickened on Thanksgiving Day, a day that deserves to be anticipated and celebrated for its own historical significance and family tradition.

But somehow, Thanksgiving dinner seems to have become a rushed affair with people impatient to get to the shopping center and the "can't live with" items that have been advertised. Many stores open at 5 or 6 in the afternoon so that shoppers can get a head start on the mad Black Friday rush.

So from Thanksgiving on through December its rush, rush, rush... eating carry-out meals because there's no time to grocery shop and cook. Then, there are all those decorations to put up, presents to wrap and cards to address. Whew! No wonder I'm ready to fall asleep at midnight on Christmas Eve.

I can't help but wonder why we have succumbed to the madness of the season instead of enjoying it the way it was in more simple times. Do you think those that rush through the season even remember the reason for this celebration?

My Cinderella Dress

When I was 12 years old my mother entered me in a 'Cinderella Contest'. The contest was open for nominations of girls 10-18 for their helpfulness and kindness.

Mama entered me because of the help I provided in caring for my little brother who had hydrocephalus and, since he couldn't walk, had to be carried or held except for the time spent in his bed. I also helped her with the housework, garden, and laundry.

I was not aware that she had nominated me until she received a notice that I was a finalist for the Cinderella title. The awards luncheon was scheduled to take place a couple of weeks later at one of the newer and fancier hotels in Paducah.

Mama made a new dress for me to wear to the luncheon. It was a dark blue iridescent taffeta that changed colors when I moved. It had a large white collar. It was the most beautiful thing I'd ever seen!

The day of the luncheon was a bright, beautiful fall day. The table was a long one and there were about six girls with the person who had nominated them sitting around it. As I recall, the food was good and I was especially intrigued by the flowers and lovely dishes.

The contest initiators made a welcoming speech and then introduced each girl by reading the letter of nomination. I was so proud standing there in my beautiful dress.

I didn't win the Cinderella award but came in second. I received several gifts and lots of congratulations. My mother was so happy! I was excited and felt special knowing how much my helping mama meant to her.

That was reward enough for me!

Dolly

My cousin Patricia lived on a houseboat with her parents and five or six siblings. The houseboat was moored alongside the shore of the Ohio River, just down from where the ferry boat docked after its river crossing.

Of course the shore was nothing but dirt and scrubby brush, but there were trees growing on the hill which rose sharply above the shoreline. It was on that hillside that Patricia and I played when our family visited her family on Sunday afternoons.

We would run up the hill, kicking up dust with our bare feet as we ran. When we came to a level spot about halfway up the hill, we would stop to run around and play our games. We had a friend Dolly who always joined us there.

Now Dolly was an odd sort, taller than us and very skinny; you might even describe her as stick thin. We ran around, singing and dancing with Dolly as the hot afternoon wore on toward evening. We sang "Dance with the Dolly with the Hole In Her Stocking" and we laughed as Dolly's hair, long and straight, twirled about.

But all too soon, we would hear Patricia's mother call to us, "Have you kids got my mop again?" And with that, we would have to run down the hill taking our friend Dolly back to the houseboat where Aunt Nina would mop up the water that had splashed onto the deck from passing barges.

You see, our friend Dolly was not real; she was not a real girl at all... she was a string mop that was kept on the houseboat deck for spills and splashes. Dolly's hair was

87

really the twisted strings of a wet mop, and her tall skinny body was the mop handle.

After Aunt Nina wiped up the water, she would hand Dolly back to us, and up the hill we would go, Patricia, me and our friend Dolly.

What wonderful and happy days!

Exposé at the Courthouse

There was a courthouse in the middle of town, and by small-town standards; it was a very nice building. It was bordered on all four sides by streets, so the square where it sat was considered the center of town.

Main Street ran past the front of the building and the street that bordered the back was where the horses and wagons were tied on a busy Saturday morning. The streets bordering both sides showcased the businesses that made up the main part of town. There was also a Greyhound Bus Station where busses discharged and picked up passengers every afternoon. In addition, the busses delivered a bundle of *The Paducah Sun Democrat*, a daily newspaper printed in Paducah. The busses also carried other small packages/freight.

There were large trees in the square that provided shade for the old men who occupied the benches that lined one side of the building. The men were there all day, Monday through Saturday. A man named Andy seemed to be the leader of the group. At the time, I thought he was pretty old but now when I think back, he was probably only 50 or so.

The remarkable thing about these old men was that they all looked pretty much alike; they wore long-sleeved shirts with faded overalls, and each of them had an old hat pulled down to shade their eyes as they watched the day flow past them. I think they all chewed tobacco, at least Andy did; there was always a tell-tale brown stain on his chin.

My friend Flora had a paper route. After school each day, she would walk the couple of blocks from school to the courthouse pulling her brother's little red wagon behind her. Leaving the wagon under one of the big trees in the courthouse yard, she would go across the street to the bus station and get the bundle of papers. Then under the watchful eyes of the old men on the bench, she would roll the papers and place them in the wagon, ready for delivery. Sometimes I would help her.

This was around 1948 and all the women wore girdles. One particular day that summer, I slipped Mama's well-worn girdle out of her dresser drawer and wore it to school. I planned to return it to her drawer when I got home and she would never know that I had worn it.

That day I had on a yellow blouse and a broomstick skirt with a floral print. The skirt was made from a printed feed sack. It was gathered onto the waistband and fastened with a button. No zipper. Since it was summer, I did not wear a slip.

I was helping Flora roll the papers and after we'd been working for a while, I straightened up, and my skirt fell to the ground! The button had popped off. There I stood with the skirt pooled around my feet; I just stood there, in shock, wearing my blouse and mama's tight little girdle. Then I bent over, grabbed the waistband of my skirt and pulled it up. Neither Flora nor I had a pin, so I had no option other than to hold it in place and head home.

Suddenly I remembered the old men that always sat there and watched us as we rolled papers. I sneaked a look at them and saw that they were all trying hard not to laugh.

I was mortified! Not only had I lost my skirt, but I had bent over with my rear end pointed directly at them when I retrieved my skirt. I had MOONED them!

The story was all over our little town the next day and everyone got a laugh out of it except for my mother, who couldn't get over that those old men had seen HER girdle! Needless to say, that was the last time I was helping Flora with her papers.

Happy Father's Day

My dad was a simple man... he worked hard and loved his family. Things were often difficult and providing for a family was challenging, especially when times were bad or work was hard to find. But somehow, he managed and even though he was essentially a worrier, he managed to hide his concerns from us.

Our home was a happy one. We always had a garden and also raised pigs and chickens, so there was always wholesome and tasty food on our table. We lived in a rented house and over the years, moved several times. Years later, when I asked mama why we had moved so often she replied that sometimes it was hard to keep the rent paid and they would look for a cheaper place. Once they bought a little house on contract, but after three or four years they had to let it go back to the owner since they couldn't afford to pay the payments.

This was in the late 40s; my youngest brother was handicapped and my parents were having medical expenses that affected their ability to pay the house payment. But neither mama nor daddy let us see that our lives were changed by these extra expenses.

Daddy was never out of work. He was a good worker and was well-liked by everyone he worked with and for. For several years he worked for Doc, a man who had moved to our little town from Texas and owned a core drilling machine; daddy learned everything he could about core drilling. Doc's two young adult sons worked with daddy and he mentored them, teaching them about the machine but also about work ethics, honesty, and in general, how to be a good man. They worked together but were friends too.

Mama packed daddy's lunch every day. He always had a sandwich of Vienna Sausage, which were sliced long ways and placed on white bread with mayonnaise. That, to us kids, was a feast! The little cans of Vienna Sausage were only bought for daddy's lunches and never for us. I don't remember what else he would have in his lunch.

When daddy came home from work each day, he would sit down in the yard, halfway between the gravel driveway and the house, set the lunch box down beside him and pull off his work shoes. Our dog Puddler would greet him, and he would wrestle with the dog for a minute.

My sister, brother and I would be in the yard to greet him, and the minute he set the lunch box aside, one of us would open it to see if there was anything left in it. And he always left a little something there for us. Finding a corner of the sandwich was the ultimate prize! We took turns enjoying whatever leftover we found.

But my favorite thing to find in the lunch box was, and this will likely gross you out, a wad of chewing gum! He would put his gum inside the lunchbox while eating and then would more than likely put a fresh piece of gum in his mouth after eating. Here's the part that will gross you out... I would put the gum in my mouth and chew it! It tasted like smoke and I loved that taste! To this day, I can't believe I did that but at the time, it didn't seem so bad. And, oh! I did love that taste of smoke.

Daddy was affectionate to mama and to us. He was kind to Grandma who lived with us for several years and when her other sons-in-law were reluctant to give her a monthly amount so that she could live on her own, daddy somehow managed to always chip in his part.

He loved to tease and when I was growing up, my friends always liked to come to our house because he would pick at them, sing silly songs to us and tease everyone.

I only saw daddy cry a few times. Once when my little brother died; once when I nominated mama for Mother of The Year and she won; and once when mama was in the hospital and he was so worried about her.

In later years, after all the kids were married and gone, he and mama became very close. They enjoyed being together and were very happy. He loved their house, and he took excellent care of the yard and outbuildings. He was working outside the Sunday morning when he had the heart attack that took his life almost a week later.

After being in the hospital for 4 or 5 days after the heart attack, he was feeling so much better. That morning he sat up on the side of his bed to eat the lunch that was brought to him. Mama and I were there, and he was teasing her and bouncing up and down. She had to tell him to quiet down, but she was smiling and happy that he was so much better.

After lunch, he took a nap. We, along with my sister went out to lunch, excited and happy about the prospect of daddy's recovery. When we returned to the hospital he was still sleeping quietly, so we left, mama to her house to catch up on some things and I to start on my way back to Cincinnati.

When I arrived at my apartment hours later, my boyfriend was there in the parking lot to greet me and tell me that my daddy had died shortly after we had left him that afternoon. He had a massive heart attack and never woke from that quiet nap.

We were all devastated. He was just a month away from his 64th birthday.

He was a good husband, father and most of all, a good person. I treasure the memories I have of my childhood and the laughing, teasing daddy that saved a portion of his lunch every day for his kids to enjoy.

I remember him with a worried frown on his face, drinking coffee at the kitchen table; I remember him with a smile on his face, sitting in the yard playing with the dog; I remember him hugging me and telling me to be careful when I was driving; but most of all I remember his disappointment and tears when I was married young; I remember how he said that he had wanted for me to be a teacher and that he would have found a way to send me to school for as many years as it took.

I remember my daddy with love; I wish I could just hug him one more time and kiss his whiskered cheek as I wished him a Happy Father's Day.

The Best Neighbor In The World

The old saying "wouldn't hurt a fly" certainly applied to my mother! She was a gentle creature and she literally wouldn't hurt a fly. She preferred hanging fly paper strips to a flyswatter. No smashed flies around our house, but there were several curly, sticky, gummed paper strips where unsuspecting flies were captured and died in what often appeared to be a mid-flight position.

But, like so many things, there can be an exception. One day mama decided that she would like to have chicken and dumplings for supper but, since it was the middle of the day, there was no one there to kill the chicken for her; well, that is, there was no one there but her.

She knew how it was done; she'd seen daddy and others do it many times... you just caught the unlucky chicken and then you did one of two things, you either wrung its neck or laid it across the chopping block and grabbed the axe. The chopping block method was messy and, to her thinking, awfully cruel. She decided that she would wring its neck; that would be quick and clean. She thought she could manage that.

Going into the chicken yard, she grabbed a nice plump hen and then went into the side yard, by the garage, where she took a firm stance, got a good grasp on the chicken's neck and flipped her wrist the way she's seen daddy do it.

Nothing happened, so she flipped her wrist again, and again, and again, but with no success. This repeated flipping looked exactly the same as if she were cranking a

Model T Ford. Finally, realizing that she, 34, wasn't going to kill the chicken this way, she turned it loose where it staggered around the yard like a drunken sailor, dizzy from all the flinging around. She didn't have the heart to attempt the chopping block method. She began to cry as her plans for a chicken dinner faded away.

There she stood, wiping her wet eyes with her apron, watching the poor chicken as it wobbled and careened across the yard. Then she heard a woman's voice and turned to see Viola, the neighbor who lived across the little road that ran between the two houses. Viola, surveying the scene being played out in the yard, walked up to mama, put her hand on mana's arm and gently said, "Here, I'll show you how it's done."

Viola then walked over to the chicken whose balance had improved somewhat, grasped it firmly around the neck and sharply flicked her wrist, just once. The chicken drooped, its broken neck evident. Mama was amazed, it looked so easy and it was definitely much more humane that the chopping block. She hugged Viola, took the dead chicken from her and walked over to the pot of boiling water where she would begin the process of scalding the chicken and plucking the feathers.

This was the first step toward making that pot of chicken and dumplings that she would proudly put on the table for supper. As she worked, she couldn't help but wonder if this might not be the first 'drunk' chicken she'd ever cooked and eaten.

Although I can't be certain, I think it's safe to say that mama never tried killing a chicken again. And, just to make things perfectly clear, for her money, Viola was the best neighbor in the world!

It was a Very Good House

It didn't look like much when we bought it, the yard was overgrown, bushes needed a trimming and tunnels where moles had traveled riddled the lawn. The poor little 1960's ranch house sat there on the slope, looking sad and really in need of someone to love it. And love it we did!

Before long, the lawn was green and cut in diagonal stripes, the bushed were trimmed and amazingly, there were no mole trails in sight. The previously sad-looking house now sat proudly and sported bright red geraniums in the three wrought iron boxes that hung across the porch railing and three more that hung beneath the bedroom windows.

The transformation continued into the house. The Harlequin light fixtures and sculpted turquoise carpet that had graced the foyer and living room were gone, replaced now with fixtures that complimented the space and shining hardwood floors reflecting the morning light. And sunlight streamed through the new ANDERSEN kitchen windows, warming us as we sat at the breakfast table.

But the best thing and the thing we probably loved most about the house were the closets... yes, the closets! Big ones, little ones, some with shelves, some with bars for hanging and even some under the basement steps for bulky things. There was a dressing room with four additional closets and in addition, there was a large cedar closet for winter clothes. It was heaven having storage space, and soon everything had found its home.

Thirty-one years later, when the time came to move into a condo, we were shocked at the amount of stuff in all these wonderful closets. There was stuff everywhere and lots of it! It was in every nook and cranny – boxes and boxes of stuff, much of it stuff we didn't even know we still had. It was downright distressing. What would we do with all of it?

After several days and countless trips from the house to the condo, the boxes were piled high, really high in the condo garage. There wasn't even space for the car!

Now, looking back, I realize that all those closets, regardless of their size or shape, whether they were drywall or cedar, shelved or with bars for hanging were one of the best things about the house, but I have also come to realize that they were, in all likelihood, the worst thing about the house. That siren call of open shelves invited the purchase of things we didn't need and possibly never even used. It was so easy to stick something in a closet instead of throwing it away.

Although I loved having all those closets, I must admit that having fewer closets would definitely have eliminated a lot of work later on. But for now, I'll just grab my writing bag out of the hall closet and head out. OOPs! I have to move some stuff to get to my bag… Oh well, some things never really change, do they?

I'll Never Forget Those Shoes

It was a sunny Saturday morning, and daddy and I were going to Paducah to buy new shoes for me. The year was 1947 or '48 and I was eleven, almost twelve years old. At that time, each of us kids had two pairs of shoes, one pair for every day and one pair for Sunday, and it was time to replace my Sunday shoes.

I was excited about two things that morning, first about getting new shoes and second, about spending the morning with daddy, who would be much easier to talk into getting what I wanted than what mama would have been. I thought it was very lucky for me that mama had sent him to get my new shoes.

Paducah was about an hour's drive from our house in Marion and my excitement started to build as soon as we pulled away from our house. It continued to build as we made our way steadily down highway 60.

When we arrived in Paducah, daddy found a parking spot, fed nickels into the parking meter, and we began the short walk to Main Street and the stores. As we waited for the light to change so we could cross the street, we noticed several people going in and out of the Walgreens store that was located on the corner right across from where we stood. There were also quite a few people walking up and down the street. I had never seen this many people shopping in our little town and was amazed at the sight.

Even though I noticed the people moving about, I was busy looking up the street at the stores, searching for one that looked like it might have shoes in it. We began our stroll up the street toward the river passing by a large department store with beautiful things in the window. There were stylish dresses, purses and gloves for ladies and frilly dresses for little girls. There were also some household items. It looked to me like a wonderful place, and I hoped that someday I would go in there to look around.

We also noticed several other stores but then, right there in front of me, I saw it! The store sat back from the sidewalk and had large plate glass windows running alongside the walkway that led into the store. But what caught my eye was the display in one of the big windows. It was filled, absolutely filled with ballet slippers!

There were slippers in every color I could imagine. They were all the same style, soft, flat ballet slippers with a small string tie at the front. Oh my... I couldn't believe my eyes. It was everything I could ever have dreamed of, right there in the window, beautiful ballet slippers!

"Daddy, daddy, look at these beautiful shoes. They are exactly what I want... can we go in and look? Please?"

"Are you sure that's what you want?" he asked.

I nodded yes and we walked into the store.

As we entered, a middle-aged man approached and asked if he could help us. Daddy told him that we were looking for Sunday shoes for me and that I liked the ones in the window. The man turned his attention to me and asked what color I would like to see. That was hard to decide... they were all so beautiful. Should I get red ones, black ones or maybe even a tan? We walked outside and looked in the window so I could make up my mind. "I want the green ones," I told him.

He went into a back room and came back with a box that held the green ballet slippers. I thought they were the most wonderful things I'd ever seen. I put them on and, feeling quite festive and pretty, I twirled around a couple of times, watching my feet in the small mirror. Daddy was not saying anything; he just stood there watching me. I said, "I want these shoes." He asked if I was sure and I said, "Yes." The salesman asked if I wanted to see another color before I made up my mind and I said, "No, I want the green ones." Daddy paid for the shoes, and we left the store, heading home.

When we got home, I ran to show mama my new shoes. She was not able to hide the look of shock and dismay that showed on her face when I opened the box. Then her look changed to one of irritation, and she turned to daddy.

"Raymond, why on earth would you buy a pair of shoes like this for her?"

Daddy looked uncomfortable as he answered, "Because that's what she wanted."

"But, green shoes! You'll have to take them back and get different ones."

I stood there listening, feeling my beautiful new shoes slipping away from me. I started to cry. "Please mama, can I keep them? I love them so much."

Mama stood there looking not only irritated but also tired and mussed from her morning's work. She looked at me, then looked at daddy but then she looked back at me, standing there with tears in my eyes, clutching the green shoes to my chest.

"Okay, you can keep them," she said. "And you're going to wear them, wear them till they fall off your feet so you'd better like them a whole lot."

I was overjoyed and I ran to the back porch where daddy had enclosed one end, making a small bedroom for me. I took the shoes out of the box and put them under my bed, placing them so that the toes peeked out where I could see them every time I walked into the room. Several times that day, I walked back there just to glance at those beautiful shoes and thought how lucky I was to have something so grand.

Every day I would proudly re-position them so that the toes were always peeking out and anyone coming into my room would see them. I was so proud of them. But unfortunately, my pride began to falter as time went on. I soon found that it was very hard to find a dress or skirt that looked nice with green shoes. Most colors just didn't seem to go well with green or at least not with that bright shade of green and when I placed them under my bed, they were no longer in a prominent position, but were scooted back far enough that I didn't have to look at them. I grew to dislike them and was embarrassed to wear them.

I wore those shoes. In fact, I wore them until they started getting ratty looking, and it was once again time for me to get new dress shoes. This time it was mama who took me to buy shoes. One of the happiest days of my life was the day I was able to say goodbye to those green shoes.

But I think I learned a valuable lesson from those shoes and it is this, "Be careful what you wish for because you might just get it and then wish you hadn't."

Let There Be Weddings!

"That's not my ring!" I said loudly. Fr. Don, standing directly in front of me, held out a ring that looked nothing at all like the wedding band I had given him before the ceremony began. Smiling broadly, he handed the ring to AL so that he could slip it on my finger. It was a lovely ring; a gold band with diamond baguettes across the top of it, and it fit my finger perfectly. But, where was my old wedding band, the one that I had worn for several years and treasured?

It was the evening of November 30, 1993, and we were in the Chapel at St. Antoninus Church with Fr. Don performing not only a marriage ceremony but also bringing me into the church. That evening I had my first communion and my first (and only) confession. I didn't have to be baptized since I had previously been baptized in both the Methodist and Baptist churches.

Fr. Don had recommended that we have a wedding ceremony in the church since we had initially been married in a civil ceremony by a local judge who was also a friend. The wedding took place in a private dining room at The Westin Hotel in September 1981. We had only eight friends and the judge there for the wedding and the wonderful dinner that followed. We even had a beautiful wedding cake.

Getting back to 1993 and our second wedding, we had Al's mother, two sisters and their husbands there to witness the ceremony, and then we all, including the Priest, went to dinner to raise a glass and celebrate.

So, you may be wondering which wedding we celebrate? The first one of course since that marks our years together.

Now that I've told you about my weddings, let me share some other wedding stories that stick in my mind...

Once when we were traveling and had stopped down in Tennessee at a Shoney's restaurant, a pickup truck pulled up beside us in the parking lot. As we were walking into the restaurant, the truck's door opened and a woman stepped out. She was wearing a floral printed dress, a hat and had a large corsage on her shoulder. Then, behind her came a little girl of about six who was also in a very fluffy dress with a large ribbon in her hair and then... a bride emerged! She had on a long white wedding gown and a short veil covered her ponytail. She was carrying a bouquet. Then, the new groom got out of the truck. He was wearing a plaid shirt buttoned up to his throat, a tie, and new buckle overalls! Then the wedding party entered the restaurant and got in line for the buffet. Everyone in the restaurant watched in amazement as they proceeded to have their celebratory wedding dinner.

Another funny story that I can share is that my brother-in-law, who was not catholic but was marrying a catholic girl, fainted as he knelt at the side altar in the church. After he was revived, the wedding went on.

And my brother, who had dressed for his wedding in the apartment that he and his new bride would be moving into, had forgotten to bring dark socks along with the tux he would be wearing. He had to wear the socks that he had on when he arrived there to get dressed. They were pink, and when he knelt, they were in full view of the guests. Everyone got a big laugh out of that.

And, oh yes, back to my wedding ring... I now wear both my original ring from 1981 and the second one from 1993. They look great together!

A Night To Remember

It was, without a doubt, the most horrible and the most frightening sound I had ever heard. It started as a low moaning sound, like someone was in pain and then slowly grew into a high-pitched sound that I, with my limited ability to describe a sound, could only imagine that it was how keening sounded.

The sad, pain-filled sound woke me and, as I lay there and listened to it go on and on, I began to feel extremely fearful for my safety. It went on for such a long time that I began to feel that I would lose my sense of reality if it didn't stop. It also sounded very close to the room where I lay, scared out of my wits.

I had flown out to Los Angeles earlier that day to visit an old friend. After she and her first husband were divorced, she had met and later married a man from California and had frequently invited me to come out and visit them. So finally, here I was, enjoying our being together and catching up on our friendship. It turned out that her son was also there, on leave from the Army. He and my son had been friends, and it was also nice to see him again.

At midnight, after a good dinner and a couple of glasses of wine, I was ready for bed and headed to my room. It was down the hall from the kitchen and almost directly across from a bathroom. It was a very small room and had only a twin-sized bed, a small chest and a chair for furnishings. There really wasn't room for anything else in there. There also were no windows, so it was rather dungeon-like and with my claustrophobia, I really wasn't very comfortable with these accommodations. Thankfully I was only planning to stay two nights there.

When I turned the lamp off, it was very dark in the room, another thing I wasn't happy with since I like to be able to see where I'm going if I get up in the night. It took me a while to fall asleep in this small dark room.

I don't think I'd been asleep for long when I heard it... that low moaning. Then, as I lay there awake, wondering if someone was sick, it became louder and more of a wailing sound. I felt scared. I could hear sounds, and then heard a man's voice mumbling something over and over between the sounds. For a while, I felt sure that someone had broken into the house and I began to fear for our lives.

Then I remembered that her son had recently returned from Vietnam and I remembered all the things I had heard about the condition of some of these soldiers and how they used drugs.

I didn't dare open the door to the hallway since I didn't know what I would find. I lay there, becoming more scared by the minute and, for the first time in my life; I felt that I was going to die. The sounds were louder and longer and closer and closer together, almost at a fever pitch. I was so terribly afraid and prayed to God for protection.

Before long, I heard someone in the hall, then after a moment, I heard the sound of glass breaking. I heard a long wail followed by the sound of something or someone falling. Then silence. I lay there and finally drifted off, feeling that whatever had been going on was done for the night.

When I heard my friend's voice and movements, I knew it was morning. I got up, dressed, packed my bag and went out to the kitchen, where she and her husband were drinking coffee at the small table. They were friendly and talkative, but they both looked as if they hadn't slept at all. Nothing was said about the sounds during the night. I felt they were embarrassed about it, so I also didn't mention it. However, I told them that I had decided that I would leave that morning and asked if they could arrange to get me to the airport. They said yes, and I think they felt relieved. I certainly felt that way!

That was at least 45 years ago. I never heard from that friend again. I don't know if her son was deployed again, if he recovered or if he eventually killed himself. I did hear from another friend later that she and her husband had divorced. What a shame. She deserved a happy life and quite possibly never found it.

An Eventful Year in My Life

The summer of 1945 was a hot one. I had turned nine in April that year, my brother was seven and my little sister was just 5. And, in addition to the three of us, mama was several months pregnant with her fourth child.

My grandma Evie lived with us and helped mama around the house and with us kids. She was especially attentive to my cute, spoiled little sister who, without doubt, was grandma's favorite. Daddy drove our only car to work every day so even though mama could drive, we had no way to go anywhere during the week.

The sun was blistering hot every day and all the grass had turned brown from lack of rain. We looked for cool places to play, finding relief under the spreading leaves of our June apple tree and on the steps that led into our underground cellar.

Three important things happened to me that summer. First, I was bitten by a snake in July. The snake had been coiled in the shady area at the bottom of our cellar steps, and I had evidently stepped on him as I ran down the stairs. I saw him draped across my foot when I looked down to see what I had stepped on. Horrified, I kicked my foot and flung the snake across the cellar floor. My brother started screaming, but I just stood there, too shocked to do anything.

Daddy rushed me to the doctor's office, where they quickly lanced the two fang marks and drew blood until it turned from the black iridescent venomous blood to a bright red and signaled that the venom was gone from my bloodstream. Only then did the doctor speak. He looked at daddy and said, "It's a good thing you got her here when you did, a few more minutes and it might have been too late."

That evening all the men in the neighborhood had a snake hunt and found a hole at the side of our house and another at the foot of those steps. They blocked the lower hole and poured boiling water down the other one. The next morning a snake that fit my description was found in our yard. That gave us some comfort.

Thinking back, I realize now how frightening that must have been for mama, who was so big with her pregnancy that she couldn't bend over to tend to my foot that day. She had me climb up onto the three-foot-tall cistern casing that was in our kitchen so she could tie a dish towel tourniquet just above my knee. The doctor said that was probably what had saved my life that day.

The second important thing that happened to me that summer was connected to WWII.

We lived in a small town in western Kentucky and then, in 1945, there were no TVs and no daily newspapers, only a local weekly paper. We did have a radio at our house but I don't ever remember seeing my parents sit down to listen to the news, although I'm sure they did.

My Uncle Tom was in the Navy and on a ship that had some Japanese prisoners on it. He had sent home a picture of one of these prisoners, and I became very fearful of the Japanese when I saw that picture. I would often sit on our back porch, which looked out over the chicken lot, the vegetable garden and then to a wooded area and I could imagine the Japanese coming out of the woods, up to our house and onto the porch where I sat. I thought they would surely kill us all. I would sit there on the floor, knees drawn up to my chin and watch the woods for long periods at a time. I felt very scared despite mama's assurance that they were far away and that they would not come to our house. Finally, daddy managed to convince me that we were safe.

The third thing that happened was a joyful event and not something that was scary or that made me fearful at the time. However, the fear came later.

On September 15, 1945 my youngest brother was born. He was named Robert Lee, and he was an absolutely beautiful, perfect baby with a ready smile and eyes that were like silver. We were all so excited and loved our baby brother.

The fear began to fill us all about three months later when he was diagnosed with hydrocephalus, a medical condition that was not curable at the time. There was not a viable surgical solution and nothing known that could alter the flow of his spinal fluid and make him well. The doctors predicted he would not live more than two years at the very most.

He was an incredible child, and he lived to be nine years old, the age I had been when he was born.

Yes, 1945 was a very eventful year for me.

Music

The chorus was fantastic. A piano accompanied the voices blending gloriously in a variety of musical selections. The first three numbers were from the opera, the next several from the theater and stage and, finally, selections from three or four different, well-known and highly-regarded composers were featured.

The first selection on the program was The Anvil Chorus from a Verdi opera. I was already getting tears in my eyes from the beauty of this piece by the time they were halfway through it. And when the voices rose, I was filled with emotion and joy. Actually, they had me from the first note!

There was a selection from Madame Butterfly and one from Carmen, all extremely well done. Two very talented soloists added their rich tones to the chorus on a couple of these pieces.

The chorus then offered show tunes, one of them being 'As Time Goes By'. That did me in! Memories of the happy times my husband and I have shared surfaced and caused tears to fall. Seeing my tears, my friend who had invited me to this concert simply placed her hand on my arm and left it there for a few heartbeats, letting me know that she was there for me.

This music gave me such joy but also brought tears with its beauty and meaning.

So, the question comes to mind, does the music set our mood or does our mood set the music?

My Special Friend

I had a very special friend during two summers. It was 1945 and 46, and I was nine and ten years old at the time.

My grandma lived several miles out of town in a small house that sat at least a couple of miles away from the main road. There were woods all around it, and the nearest neighbor was at least a quarter of a mile away. It was, at least to someone my age, very lonely at her house.

I spent a week with Grandma each of those two summers. Throughout the day, Grandma and I listened to the soaps on her little radio, and I helped her prepare the cloth strips for the rag rugs that she made. It was peaceful and comforting there in the little house during the day.

But at night, it was a different story. The nights were so terribly dark, and you could hear the cries and other sounds of the animals that lived in the woods surrounding the house.

Grandma and Grandpa slept in the one-bedroom that was in the house. I had to sleep on a soft pallet that was laid out on the living room floor. Once Grandma got me settled in my pallet bed at night, she would leave the room, taking the oil lamp with her, leaving the room pitch black all around me. I was scared.

But I found a friend that helped me through those dark nights. It wasn't an imaginary friend, but something real. The Seth Thomas clock that sat on the living room mantle became my friend! In the darkness, I could hear the steady TIC-TOC, TIC-TOC all night long. It chimed on the hour and the half-hour and that was music to my young ears! I was no longer alone and scared in the dark... I had the clock with me. It was my friend, and I could sleep with the darkness and the animal sounds around me, knowing that something was in the room with me.

When Grandma died, my daddy got the clock and he promised it to me someday. That day came when he died in 1979, and my old friend the clock came to live with me. It works great and still goes TIC-TOC, TIC-TOC and still chimes on the hour and half hour. I find myself listening for it at odd times during the day and night even though my house is well lighted at night, and I hardly ever hear any animal sounds.

My friend the clock lives on and will hopefully befriend another scared little girl someday.

Chicken Dinner

In the middle of the 1970's, I started a new job where I was an office manager and bookkeeper for a small insurance agency. One of our main clients was a gentleman who owned a company that built river barges.

Since his company was located in Indiana, he often made a trip to Cincinnati before heading back. Generally, my boss would invite the gentleman to his home for dinner when he was in town.

One particular time, my boss asked me if I would make dinner for them since his wife was out of town visiting her parents. Of course, but with quite a bit of trepidation, I said yes.

I decided I would make Chicken Tarragon since I had made it previously and it was edible.

When the big evening came, my boss and his client arrived and sat down in my living room with drinks while I rustled around in the kitchen, putting the finishing touch to our dinner. I had a glass of wine and then had then another while I was working. I cooked the chicken, adding tarragon to the sauce as directed.

Obviously, I had more wine than I needed since, when I served the meal, it was awful. Everything was good except for the chicken. There was an abundance of tarragon in the sauce over the chicken, and it couldn't be eaten without a struggle.

Evidently, I had continued adding tarragon long after it was needed. I guess I had added more as my wine consumption increased.

Desert was good – nobody died from the bad meal… and the client stayed with our company.

But I haven't tried that dish since, and I am not fond of any dish that has tarragon in it since that taste somehow brings up a bad memory!

The Book

The world was pretty small for a little girl growing up in a western Kentucky town with a population of 3200 people in the late 30's and 40's. Unlike in today's world, there were no televisions at that time and only a local, weekly newspaper which mostly contained county news.

The nearest cities were Paducah, Kentucky located forty miles southwest of our little town and Evansville, Indiana, which was about sixty miles northwest. As you can imagine, trips to either of these cities did not occur with any frequency and were often made by women and children on a Greyhound Bus since the men drove the family car to work every day. These bus trips could be a long and harrowing experience for the woman traveling with children who wiggled, cried, slept and sometimes even fought with a sibling during the long ride.

So to me, as a depression-era child living in this small world, school was the most wonderful thing I could imagine. It opened up my world to include things I wouldn't have dreamed of. Naturally curious, I loved everything about school but especially the books.

The most incredible and life-changing thing happened to me in the third grade when I opened my World Geography book. There were color pictures of people in other countries tending their fields, enjoying games and sports and even pictures of homes and family life. I saw how people dressed, the foods they grew and ate, and I was enthralled with the pictures of cities.

I was especially drawn to pictures of skyscrapers in New York and Chicago; I was mesmerized by pictures and descriptions of the ballet, the opera and theater. Of course we had a movie theater in our little town but what I learned in that geography book was that there was so much more than a movie theater in other places. I yearned to see and experience those things; see those buildings, and meet those people

It was several years before I lived those dreams, but I did see the skyscrapers in Chicago, New York and Boston, as well as other cities. I attended operas, and was thrilled by the beauty of ballet. Everything I experienced was even better than I had dreamed of since the third grade.

So now, many years later, I can look back on that third-grade classroom and feel again the wonder and excitement of my discoveries and the beauty I found in that geography book. There is no question in my mind that, apart from the Bible, that geography book has had the most impact on my life. Because of it, I have searched out new things, met people in other countries and have learned more about other cultures.

I also had another memorable experience in the third grade while leaning over to get a pencil that had fallen on the floor but... that's a story for another time.

Musical Notes

Somewhere in a dark corner of my mind where obscure and often irrelevant facts and thoughts reside, I found what I think is an appropriate quote about music. It simply states, "Music is nectar for the soul."

Now I don't know whether I've quoted this correctly or even if it is a legitimate quote but somewhere in this dark little corner where I found it, something tells me that it is correctly stated and that it was once said by someone who was or should be, remembered for their witticisms.

Regardless of the validity of this quote, I like it and believe it to be true. If I had made it up, I would probably have said, "Music feeds the soul and calms our being." I do believe that music plays an important role in our lives.

As a matter of fact, music has been important to people since biblical days when harps and other instruments were played in adoration of the king, at weddings, and other celebrations. Shepherds often played the flute to calm their sheep. Have you ever read a book or viewed a movie that didn't mention music in some way?

Music fuels our creativity. It is well known that people come up with better ideas when listening to happy, upbeat music played softly and we feel a rush of energy when a powerful song is heard enabling one to perform at a greater speed or for a longer period of time. Think about it, the song, 'Let's Get Physical' is often paired with exercise programs and Ravel's composition, 'Bolero' is jokingly associated with sexual activity.

Music also lulls us to sleep, decreases levels of stress, and is sometimes used to reduce anxiety and lessen the need for pain medication in a patient before surgery. And oddly, researchers have found that surgeons work more efficiently and accurately when the music of their choice is played in the background.

Just think how our moods can change from hearing a particular song; how a memory can surface when a certain melody fills the air around us. And, strange as it may seem, there is one song that makes me feel nauseous every time I hear it. I know that's weird and I don't understand how it happens but it does happen. I don't know why but I imagine it is tied to something or sometime when I didn't feel well or something unpleasant happened. That song is 'Wind Beneath My Wings'. It really is a pretty song with words that normally provoke memories of someone very important to the listener.

I've often heard the question, "Does music set the mood or does the mood set the music?" I don't think there's a hard and fast answer to this but for me I would say that both scenarios are correct. How many times do we choose a blues number when we're feeling down or nostalgic? Listening to something upbeat or fun can enhance a good mood and of course we've all got our favorite romantic song.

I wonder, if we each sat down and made a list of our favorite musical genre, favorite songs, favorite artist, favorite bands, and even our favorite instruments, what would that list say about us?

I think you could safely say that I am someone who loves all music, from classical, big bands, and country to the old Deep South bluesy songs that stir my soul.

Baptized Again

I was baptized in the Methodist Church when I was about 12 years old. Then, in 1965, I was baptized in the First Southern Baptist Church of Hammond, Indiana. I was then 29 years old. The pastor was a very tall (over 6 feet by 3 or 4 inches), lean and lanky man who had come there from somewhere in Texas.

The church had a baptismal font located behind the pulpit. There was a wall behind the pulpit that hid the font from view. A large opening in the wall allowed the congregation to see only the upper body of the person being baptized and the preacher. The opening was covered with a large picture except for the times when there were baptisms taking place.

I had been told to go to the dressing room located downstairs in the church when the regular church service was getting close to the end on that Sunday morning. There, in the dressing room, someone would me get ready for baptism.

In 1965, BIG hair was in style so my blonde hair was teased and sprayed to the point where a typhoon couldn't have moved it. The top was teased very high, the back and sides were teased into a fluffy flip, and the whole thing had been sprayed to the 'nth degree. I was wearing a blue printed summer shirtwaist dress with a half-slip, panties, bra, and sandals with no stockings. A picture of fashion!

Well... the preacher's wife and another lady were waiting for me when I went downstairs. I should have known this was not going to be easy when one of the ladies asked where I had put my dry underclothes. I replied that I didn't know I was supposed to bring a change of underclothes with me and so I didn't have any. When they heard that, they were beside themselves.

With only a short time left to get me ready, they tried desperately to figure out what to do and quickly came up with a plan. The pastor's wife (a lady who was much larger than me) would go to the parsonage, which was behind the church and get a pair of her underpants for me to be baptized in. The underpants she brought back were several sizes too big, and they had to pin them over so they wouldn't fall off.

We still had the dilemma of no dry bra or slip. They decided that I would have to keep my undergarments dry, and that meant I would have to go into the water not wearing these items. This evidently was a terrible thing and something they hadn't had to deal with before. After some thought, they decided that I could wear two baptismal robes and nobody would know that I wasn't wearing a bra and slip. So, with fingers crossed, they suited me up with two robes and a pair of the preacher's wife's underpants. I was ready at last.

When I went up the stairs to the little area beside the baptismal font, there were four or five men waiting there with the preacher. He said that since I was the only woman being baptized that day, I would go first. O.K. We were ready to begin. Now when you looked at the baptism from out in the congregation, it seemed like the preacher and the person being baptized just slowly walked into the shallow pool; the person was gently laid back in the water, and then they walked from the baptismal font. It looked so quick and easy!

Much to my surprise, there were about three or four steps that led down into the font so the water was not as shallow as I thought. However, when the preacher walked down into the font, the water only came up to his hips or thereabouts, so it still didn't look too bad. Even though I had a fear of water, I was sure I could do it with no problem.

Now what I didn't take into account that day was that he was well over six feet tall and I was a mere five feet and six inches. When I walked into the water, it kept rising on me till it came up to my chest. I knew I was in trouble then. But what I didn't know was that the worst was yet to come.

When I walked down into the font and stood in front of the preacher, he whispered down to me, "*Where is your handkerchief?*" I whispered back, "*What handkerchief?*" He said, "*Didn't anyone tell you to bring one?*" I knew then that I had a problem, I just didn't know what. I whispered back, "*No.*" There must have been panic showing on my face, but I knew I couldn't back out at that point.

Still whispering, he said, "*Oh well, just fold your hands like this* (he demonstrated the way to fold them) *and then, when I put you back into the water, take a deep breath and hold your nose with your thumb and forefinger, no one will notice that.*" I nodded that I understood.

All the while, the congregation was watching.

He began the baptism ritual by saying whatever words he normally said (I couldn't tell you a single word of it because I was too nervous about the "take a deep breath and hold your nose" part), and then he took hold of my hands and began to slowly lower me backwards into the water. Following his instructions, I took a deep breath and pinched my nose but unfortunately, I did it just as my head went into the water. Much to my horror, I was strangling on the water I had inhaled! Panicked and struggling for breath, I began to cough and flail around in the water. After what seemed like an eternity, he helped me to stand upright and turned me toward the stairs leading out of the font.

Still coughing and with water streaming down my face and leaving a wet trail on the floor, I hurriedly escaped back down to the dressing room, got out of the wet robes and the borrowed underwear, got into my clothes and left as quickly as I could. I expected to see my family waiting there on the sidewalk, but no one was there.

I walked to the corner, hair dripping but still standing high on my head, and then I saw them waiting a half-block down the street. I hurried to catch up with them, and when I got there, my son turned to me and said, "Mom, you sounded like a seal." My husband agreed and chimed in with, "All we could see was the preacher's face and your feet coming up out of the water in front of him. There was all sort of splashing and coughing. It was embarrassing."

I couldn't believe it! *They* were embarrassed? That's why they hadn't waited for me? I was mortified about what had happened and hurt that they hadn't even waited for me to come out of the church. I looked and felt a mess.

I didn't return to church for a month after that event. Finally, one of the ladies in the congregation called me one day and said they'd been missing me at church. I made some lame excuse, and then she said, "Honey, if you're embarrassed about what happened when you got baptized, don't be. We've had worse things than that to happen." That made me feel somewhat better, and I did go back to church the next week.

There's more to my religious history. But, don't worry… I didn't have to be baptized again.

A Trip to Remember

A trip from Hammond, Indiana to Western Kentucky in the 1950's meant several hours of traveling down Highway 41, which was a popular north-south route. The heavily traveled road began in Michigan's Upper Peninsula and ended in Miami, Florida.

Driving through Indiana could take a long time as the two-lane road was pretty curvy and usually had a lot of trucks that slowed to navigate the curves and to accommodate the many access roads that fed onto the highway. It could be scary, especially at night. It could also be a lonely drive as it meandered through rural areas, and there was little to see along the way.

It wasn't unusual to see hitch-hikers along the highway, and we frequently picked someone up. Everyone did it and it never occurred to us that it could be dangerous.

One particular hitch-hiker stands out in my mind.

It was dusk and I was driving; my husband was sitting in front with me and our three-year-old son was sleeping in the back. We saw a young man on the side of the road and stopped to offer him a ride. He climbed into the front seat, putting my husband between us. He didn't say much but seemed friendly.

After a while, I saw flashing lights come up behind me and I glanced at the speedometer. Realizing that I was driving quite a bit over the posted speed limit, I slowed and pulled over to the side of the road.

The policeman came up to the window, told me I was speeding, and asked to see my license and the car registration. He also asked me who the two passengers were and I told him that it was my husband and a hitch-hiker that we had picked up several miles back. He shined his flashlight into the car and looked at my husband, then turned the flashlight on the face of our passenger.

Without saying a word, the policeman walked around the back of the car, opened the door, shined the light onto our passenger's face again and asked him a few questions before telling him to step out of the car. He then had him put his hands on the top of the car, spread his legs, and patted him down. Then he put cuffs on him and took him over to the patrol car, where he put him in the back seat. We didn't know what was going on, but it was obvious that the policeman was much more interested in our passenger than in us or the fact that I had been speeding.

The policeman returned to our car and told us to follow him to the Justice Of The Peace located in a nearby town where we could pay our fine for speeding. He pulled away, lights flashing. We followed. After driving for a good 15 to 20 minutes, he pulled into the driveway of a large white house. The sign on the front lawn read 'Justice Of The Peace'.

He got out of his car, helped his prisoner out, and motioned for us to get out and follow him as he entered the house. We were seated in a small room with several chairs arranged along the wall. The policeman took his prisoner into an adjoining room after telling us to wait there. He said he would be back in a few minutes.

We waited for what seemed a long time but probably wasn't more than a half-hour. When he came back into the room, he told us we were free to go and advised me to 'slow it down'.

We just stood there, not sure whether we should go… we didn't quite understand what was going on. I said, "What about the speeding ticket?" He answered, "Well, I'll let you off with just a warning this time."

Confused by this turn of events, we asked what was going on and where he had taken the hitch-hiker and why.

He held the front door open for us and stepped aside so we could move onto the porch as he said, "When I looked at the face of your passenger, I thought I recognized him as someone we've been looking for all week and when I asked him to get out of the car and searched him, I felt certain he was the guy we wanted."

He then told us, "Don't pick up any more hitch-hikers… some of them are not good guys. Your passenger tonight was wanted for a serious crime and he was carrying a large and very dangerous knife. So your heavy foot on the gas pedal tonight that got my attention may have just saved your life!"

He stood and watched while we got into our car and then, as I started to drive away, he said, "Drive carefully and remember my warning about hitch-hikers."

Believe me, we did have a different view of hitch-hikers after that night, and never again offered a ride to one.

Christmas Memories

While searching through my storehouse of Christmas memories, looking for that special one, I came up with not one, but several that qualified as special.

As a child, I learned that Christmas was a time of celebrating the birth of Jesus; a time for showing the spirit of love to those around us; a time for spreading goodwill and for giving gifts. There were always colored lights strung on houses and trees and a general feeling of happiness, love, and excitement in the air. There were beautiful Christmas carols sung by the choir in our church and a stirring message by the minister.

Although our family was poor, we always had special treats during the couple of weeks surrounding Christmas. We had oranges and bananas, and there were little bowls of hard candies sitting around. The house smelled like citrus and also like the gingerbread that mama baked. We had cakes and pies and there was always float, a custard-like drink that was made with eggs, milk and sugar. The men would often put a small amount of whiskey in their glass to give it a kick. Today that drink is called Eggnog, and I think some people still "spike" it with alcohol.

One of our family traditions was to get our tree. We didn't go to a lot to buy one but rather went with Daddy into the woods where we would select a tree, he would cut it down, and we would drag it home. Our tree was usually a little scraggly, but we thought it was beautiful. After being in the warm house for a while, the intoxicating scent of evergreen co-mingled with the citrus and gingerbread scents and created a unique smell that meant Christmas to us.

Today, as I sifted through my Christmas memories, I remembered other times that were special in some way. There was the year that my first husband bought me two new sweater/skirt outfits that were wool and itched me terribly. I could hardly stand to wear them but didn't want to hurt his feelings. I can remember being at work, tugging at the sweater, trying to keep it away from my body, and I remember pulling at my half-slip to cover my skin where the skirt touched me. But they were pretty outfits, and I struggled through.

I remember Christmases with mama and daddy after all of us kids were married and living away from the little town where we grew up. Mama always had a tree, probably 3 or 4 feet tall, that sat on a table in front of the picture window in the living room. It was always a pitiful-looking thing, thin on one side and usually leaning one way or the other. She purposefully selected the worst tree on the lot because she felt sorry for it and thought that no one would buy it.

We always had a big Christmas meal at Mama's and those times will always be special to me. There was so much laughter and love when we were all together. Of course, my brother, sister, and I tried to re-create those times with our own families later in life.

In more recent years, Al and I celebrated with a Christmas Eve dinner with his family and then we would exchange our gifts when we got home. Since neither of us needed anything, we later started giving money to our church to give anonymously to a family in need. That made us happy.

Last year I spent Christmas alone and will do the same this year. While the spirit of Christmas and celebrating the birth of Jesus will always remain in my heart, it's just not the same without my husband and family with me.

Movements of a Dancer

The rhythmic tapping of feet or the graceful leaps and pirouettes are movements associated with dancers. These smooth, fluid movements which appear to be so effortless are, in reality, the result of many hours of practice and years of putting the dance first. Everything, diet, exercises, and amount of rest has been geared to keeping the dancer's body in top shape and ready for the gruelling practice sessions.

Yes, I've mentioned years of training! Very likely, the dancer we see performing today began lessons as early as age three. Some lessons began as a means of feeding a mother's dream of seeing HER CHILD perform. Can't you see her child has more talent and charm than any of the others in class?

Some of that talent is only in the mother's eyes and doesn't ever reach the child's feet. In that case, a teacher must find a way to let the parents know that their child is not a dancer.

Usually, the beginning of dance classes will incorporate tap, ballet and modern dance. Every teacher will identify the students most talented in each group and then direct that child's growth and learning process toward a specific area.

We can picture the tap dancer, a little "hoofer", complete with tuxedo, top hat, and cane. Strutting first across the stage, then dancing back across it; doing fancy cross-over steps, double taps and possibly some jumps or even splits. His patent shoes are gleaming as the dance ends, and our dancer doffs his hat to the appreciative audience. Perhaps a rising star is launched with this performance!

For the child whose talent is directed toward ballet, there is that familiar ache of pulled or strained muscles, torn ligaments and broken toenails while perfecting that pointe. Stomachs growl in accompaniment to the music, louder and louder as the number of repetitions increases.

Perspiration glistens on every part of the student's body as he works out. Finally, exhausted, he stops, cools down, dresses and goes home to rest for tomorrow's practice session. One day ballet patrons will see a sleek, graceful and beautiful performance. No perspiration to stain the carefully cut and fitted costume; no muscles crying out for relief; no sense of hunger except for the applause and love flowing from the audience when the dance is finished.

It was a long road from beginning dance class to this triumph, but was it worth it? You bet! In this moment of beauty, the audience does not know of the hard work and pain, and the dancer has forgotten it.

Poems and Haiku

I Don't Care

I told the world I didn't care
The day you went away.
I told myself I didn't miss you,
But that was yesterday.

Today it all looks different,
I know I've told a lie.
I do care and I miss you so,
Why did you say goodbye?

If you would just come back to me
And we could start anew,
I'd tell the whole wide world the truth,
How sad I am without you.

My Memories

One day I looked around and saw
That the years were rushing past;
So swiftly were they going
But, where did they go so fast?
I thought about it for a while,
Wondering how I had failed to see,
That the years were not completely gone,
They were stored in my memory.

Each passing year is stored away,
Each in its special place,
With memories of a baby's kiss,
A sudden smile, a fond embrace.

Some of these treasured memories
Are sad ones that bring tears,
But they're all precious nonetheless,
My memories of the passing years.

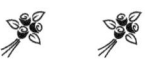

A Small Town Life

To know the fun of city life,
Exciting, loud and bright.
To feel the pulse of industry,
Furnaces glowing in the night.

I wouldn't trade it for the calm
That a small country town brings,
Where night is pierced only by the fireflies
And notes a tree frog sings.

Flying

So many lights!
Tiny flecks of brightness in the dark night.
Looking to me like a giant fistful of jewels
Strewn carelessly over black velvet.
It's stirring, and more beautiful
Than I could have ever imagined.

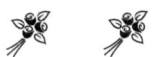

My Love

How can I describe my feelings for you?
For want of a better word, I'll call it love
But there are so many things
All tied together.
You know what I really feel
Without my saying it.
Although I may be jealous, possessive,
And even a little demanding,
Don't let my passions frighten you.
I love you, but I don't want to destroy you.

Trees

Trees, standing proud against a backdrop of blue sky,

Stretching up to touch it.

Some standing taller than others

Each one different and unique,

Calling to me with their individual beauty.

Trees, spreading their branches, some wide, some slender
and tall,

Each limb stark, stripped of its leaves,

Held fast by winter's cold breath.

Quiet in their dormancy, yet graceful in the movements

Created by the wind.

Trees, larger limbs supporting smaller ones

Lending strength and form to their beauty.

Like people, each tree has its own shape, its own
personality.

Traits hidden by summer leaves,

But revealed now in the nakedness of winter.

Summer Days

It seems like only yesterday
When we ran across the fields
Chasing horseflies and bumblebees
Stopping only to examine some new find.

A rock, a flower or maybe a clump of dirt,
Till finally we'd lie on our backs
On beds of clover
And watch the clouds drifting lazily across the sky.
Look at that one!

It looks like a fat puppy – see its ears?
And there, see the giraffe,
Its long neck waving as it drifts along
On slender legs that hardly seem to move.

My Life

The hours and days go rushing by,

The months and years, they really fly.

One day I was twelve, and every day was an adventure to
treasure.

Then, before I knew it, I was seventy,

Still finding every day exciting and new.

Each day held untold pleasure for me.

Although my mirror reflects some changes,

My heart still tells me that I'm young

And sometimes I forget to be seventy!

How did I go from twelve to seventy so quickly?

What happened to all those years that once stretched out
before me?

Years that now are dwindling?

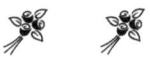

Waiting

There it lay

The robin that had flown into my window.

Now lying lifeless in a soft heap on my porch

And there, close by, sits her mate

Waiting for her to move

To fluff her wings and fly away with him.

Grandma's Front Yard

Grandma's front yard overlooked a field of hay

With a fragrance so sweet and fresh it filled me with joy.

Poppies lined the fence that separated the yard from the
hay field,

Their orange-red blossoms bobbing playfully in summer
breezes.

It was peaceful and serene there,

A shady spot enjoyed by grownups on a Sunday afternoon

While the kids played and made exciting discoveries

Of an abandoned bird's nest, a busy ant hill,

Hams hanging in the smokehouse and

Apples drying on a screen that lay high on the roof of the
old building,

Secure from hungry birds and animals.

We ate a cold supper and then kissed Grandma and
Grandpa Goodbye.

We waved back to them as Daddy drove through the gate
and across the field

That would take us to the highway and home.

Another Sunday at Grandma's house had come and gone,
recorded only in my memory now.

Fall Colors

The sweet colors of fall have arrived

And they are surely a sight to behold.

I see leaves of many colors

But mostly there are lots of reds and golds.

Then I see it…

There, on one tree that stands a little apart from the others,

Perfect leaves of butterscotch yellow,

A color so warm and soft, so soothing,

Making it easy to forget that winter will soon be here.

Our Magical Summer

We played on the bluff where thick moss grew on tree
trunks

And violets carpeted the ground.

We twisted white clover blossoms into necklaces and
bracelets

And wore them proudly.

We swung on the wooden gate that opened into the
barnyard

And we chewed on the mint leaves that grew wild along
the fence row.

We dipped our toes into the cool brown water of the pond

And we watched the horses swish away the flies with their
long tails.

Sometimes we sat on the trunk of a tree

That grew perpendicularly out over the creek bed,

And our bare feet danced in the air over the bubbling
water.

That summer was truly magical for us.

Every day was an adventure that we thought would never
end.

Yet they always ended when we heard Aunt May calling

To come in and wash up for supper.

Autumn's First Dance

They rose from the tree tops,
At least that's how it appeared.
Flying in random paths,
Not quite organized,
Yet the leader is clearly defined.
A dozen or so geese,
Silent now in first flight
They circle,
Flying low over the tree tops.
Another group,
Half as large as the first,
Rises to join them.
The group now falls into its formation,
And the honking conversation begins.
The leader turns them directly to the west,
Flying into an evening sky
That silhouettes and welcomes
These early autumn travelers.

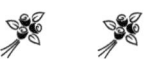

Dancing Dolly

We played on a dirt hillside,
High on the river bank
Where tree branches hung low and shaded us on hot
afternoons.

Our favorite thing to do
Was dancing around the hillside
Singing 'Dance with the Dolly with a Hole in her
Stocking'.

Aunt Nina's mop was our 'Dolly'
The mop strings magically became golden curls
That bounced and swirled around and down Dolly's back.

We spent hours there,
Running, dancing and laughing.
Our feet kicking up miniature whirlwinds in the soft
brown dirt.

All too soon, mama would call to me and it was time to
say goodbye.
Yet we knew that we'd soon spend another Sunday
afternoon
With Dolly in our favorite spot on that shady hillside.

Friends

When friends are scattered,
Only memories can fire the passion of love
Buried deep in each heart.

Vision

Misty sunlight spills through
Opening the way before me,
I can now see everything.

Caress

Wind and I as one,
Whispering all around you,
Caressing you softly.

Memories

Memories are gifts
That we can open one by one,
And enjoy over and over.

Beauty

Beauty rules every space
And fills me to capacity
Joy and love is mine.

Nature

Despite the seeming disorder
There is structure and meaning
To nature as well as to life.

Hearts

Hearts can hear things

That eyes cannot see

Yet we understand and cherish them all.

Trees

Branches gnarled and bent

Their secrets all bared

A life in retrospect.

Crocus

Clustered beneath snow's blanket

They lie in wait for spring

Gathering strength to delight us.

Birthday

Thrust now into a new place

Bright and warm and loud

To live and grow in wonder and awe.

Creativity

Thoughts spring up like weeds

Unexpected and uninvited

Some flourish, others die.

Peaceful Moments

My heart quietly listens

To the peaceful sounds around me.

I am soothed and fulfilled.

Acknowledgments

Thanks to the many friends and family who inspire me daily. Also thanks to my mother for instilling in me a love for reading and for capturing my thoughts on paper. I truly love and appreciate everyone who has encouraged and supported me throughout my life and who has loved me even when I was sometimes hard to love.

Bless you all!

About the Author

Jenny Zimmer is a writer, artist and book lover! Retired from an executive position, she spends her time doing the things she loves, which include not only writing but other activities that fuel her creative spirit and soothe her soul. She is sensitive and caring but also has a humorous side that comes out often in her short stories. She has previously published "All The Moments Are Real", available on Amazon.

www.ingramcontent.com/pod-product-compliance
Lightning Source LLC
Chambersburg PA
CBHW060226180626
46813CB00007B/2971